My Eclair, I love you!

Hers

XOXO

Dawn Ro

DAWN ROBERTSON

Hers is dedicated to:

The misfits.

The freaks.

Those who were told you will never amount to anything in life.
My own personal angel.

My Family.

The women who worked tirelessly on this novel with me. My beta readers, my editor Sarah Daltry, Rachel Mizer from Shoutlines Design for all the beautiful graphics, formatting, and the award-winning cover.

To the bloggers who have helped me with this debut including Brandelyn from Seductive Romance Reviews, Stephanie of Stephanie's Book Reports, and so many more.

If I forgot you, I am sorry!

I love you all!

Thank you for supporting my dream & don't stop believing!

PROLOGUE

"It just isn't going to work out. Ya know, long term." Daniel looked me in the eye. His emerald green eyes that I'd fallen in love with during our college English class told a different story. It wasn't about the future, or the fact that we came from much too different backgrounds. There was someone else. I had sensed it in the way he fucked me. The passion that once had been carnal was just missing.

I rolled my eyes at him and chucked up two fingers in the peace sign. "Deuces, Daniel. Get your shit, and get the fuck out." I couldn't let him see that I cared. I couldn't allow him the satisfaction of knowing my heart was breaking. I couldn't let him see me weak. I didn't let anyone see it.

"Seven, let's talk about this."

He wrapped his muscular pale arm around my waist as I tried to move across the kitchen section of my thrift shop nightmare studio apartment. I pulled away with such force that I tripped over my own bare feet.

"There isn't anything to talk about. I just want you to go." I grabbed his overpriced black leather jacket off the couch and threw it at his face with everything I had. Before contact, his arm caught it in mid-air. I was pissed. I needed him to hurt just as bad as I did.

He reached for the door, without looking back. A single tear started to form in my eye, and rage began to take over. My new determination was to hurt this bastard the way he had just crushed me.

"You were a shitty lay anyways," I screamed at him.

The door closed without an ounce of reaction from Daniel. It was amazing how he could just turn off his emotions. Erupting in a fit of rage, I threw my platform stilettos at the worn white door. When that didn't make me feel any better, I went rummaging through my cabinet in search of something with more meaning. Then I saw it. The vase. Sparkling and full of the memory of our first anniversary together. He'd bought me a dozen multi-colored roses, knowing I could never pick my favorite color when it came to the beautiful flowers. With purpose, I lifted it, hurling it across the tiny space and watching it shatter into a million sharp pieces.

There is no fucking way I am cleaning that up right now.

My bare feet pattered across the black and white tiled floor to the closet sized bathroom. Once inside, I cranked the shower as hot as the old pipes in my building would supply. Cold water poured as I stripped, starting with the plain white t-shirt that barely covered my tattooed stomach. I tugged at my yoga pants and thong, kicking them into a messy pile on the bathroom floor. I stood naked in front of the full length mirror I kept on the back of the cheap wooden door.

Steam rose from the shower, signaling that it was finally warm. I broke away from the staring contest I was having with myself in the mirror, or should I say, silently pointing out every last flaw I have? Every reason Daniel wouldn't want to be with me. Was it my scars? The tattoos I used to cover them up? Was it the fact that I wasn't a perfect size zero? Or maybe it was just the fact that my life was simply fucked up. I don't have the purebred pedigree his parents want for his bride.

My hard exterior had always been a front. Seven, the emotionally unavailable nomad, had finally opened herself up to another living soul, only to be trampled to pieces. Only once in my life had I experienced true heartbreak. The loss of Daniel stung just as bad. I cared more than I would ever admit. I'd let my walls down for him, and he had taken advantage of it.

Well marriage wasn't in my plans anyway. *So suck on that, asshole!*

What was in my plan? Fucking taking over the world! Gone would be Seven, the broken daughter of nomad hippies.

Losers who couldn't nail down a job if handed a hammer and nail. I had become everything they hated about society. But their biggest problem with me was the fact that I had actually obtained a college education. While most parents encourage their children to take the SATs and apply to colleges, I had to sneak behind their backs to better myself.

CHAPTER 1

Five Years Later

"Miss James." The intercom in my office buzzes with Olivia, my assistant's voice.

"Yes, Livie?" I answer, while finishing the last couple keystrokes on my laptop.

"Mr. Stern is here for your two o'clock."

Looking at the clock on my computer screen, I instantly grow annoyed when I see it reads quarter after one. *He's early. I normally like early, but this is just obnoxiously early. What the fuck gives?*

I pick up my phone, dialing Olivia's private extension and simmer, waiting until she answers. I shouldn't take my aggravation out on her, but I do. It is a bad habit, but she's used to it. I don't think anyone can handle me better than my personal assistant.

I blow out a breath and count in my head, calming myself down from the pending shitty mood that is brewing like a hurricane. The line clicks to life with sunshine and unicorns in her overly cheerful hello.

"He is going to have to wait. I have a couple things to wrap up before he can come back."

Slamming the phone down on the desk, I let out a sigh and make my way across the room to the bathroom to freshen myself up. After feverishly working out every detail of the single, biggest deal of my life all morning, I look like a goddamn hot mess. My blouse sleeves are rolled up past my elbows, exposing my sea of tattooed arms. Angels, flowers, and cherry blossoms peek out from under the wrinkled fabric. I am typically very careful to conceal my vast artwork at work, but unfortunately, I had been swept away into my work far too easily today.

Smoothing out the creases in my black dress pants and slipping my red leather pumps back on, I roll the white sleeves of my button up blouse back down and run my fingers through my long chestnut hair before scooping it up into a messy bun.

Last, I grab my glasses off the counter. I hate wearing them outside of the office, but I'm virtually blind without them. The black rimmed emo accents make me seem less predatory during a deal. Little do these business men know that I could eat them for breakfast. That's why, at twenty-seven years old, I virtually run one of the largest communications corporations, White-Woods Global. Alas, I really need to get to the eye doctor and fucking invest in some damn contacts. *Damn, ain't nobody got time for that!*

A chuckle escapes me, as I pull out the thick black folder containing all my notes and contracts for the buyout of Alexander Mobile. The single biggest deal of my entire career.

By this time on Friday, I will ruin Daniel Alexander as I swoop into the boardroom of his father's company and take the job he has dreamed of since he was a little boy. *How is that for karma, douche-nugget?*

Peering into the mirror once more before inviting my impending visitor back, I smack my lips together, smoothing my newly applied lipstick, and buzz Olivia. "Send Mr. Stern back, please."

Striding around the side of my desk, I make my way across

the burgundy carpet, and open the heavy cherry wood door. Plastering a fake smile across my lips for the old sucker. "Mr. Stern, how great to see you." I extend my hand in greeting.

"Likewise, Ms. James. I was pleased with the contract you sent over. I've been itching to sell my shares of Alexander Mobile for some time."

Music to my ears. Little does he know, but he is about to drop the majority of his company into my lap right before they become one of the most sought after mobile distributors in the world. But I would never tell the old man that.

"I've had some interest in Alexander Mobile for years, and the time is right." I pull out a chair, offering it to the ancient man. Unfortunately for him, he doesn't know my interest in the Alexanders goes far beyond business; it is personal. It has been personal since Daniel left me and took up with that trust-fund Barbie doll, Samantha Rockwell. Not that I even really give a shit about him anymore. This is pure revenge, the last nail in my vendetta so I can finally move on with my damn life.

"So, I take that you are pleased with all the details of the purchase? Why don't you go ahead and give me your John Hancock on a couple of these papers, and we will schedule the board meeting for two days from now. Say Friday morning bright and early?"

I pull the last contract out of my folder, sliding it across the desk while pointing with my mint-colored nails at the two X's that need his signature. The old man pulls an expensive pen out of his blazer breast pocket and scribbles his name down in both places. I let out a small sigh of relief. It's too easy, like taking candy from a baby.

"I've been looking to offload these shares for years, Ms. James. I just need to hang up my hat and retire. Thank you for helping me finally give it all up. You be good to Daniel Alexander; he is a good businessman." He slowly rises from the chair, although probably the fastest his old body will allow him anymore.

He extends his arm in my direction, and I shake with vigor before reassuring him.

"I will be sure to take care of Mr. Alexander. Thank you for being such a gracious businessman, Mr. Stern." I flash him a million dollar smile. Or maybe I should say a sixty million dollar smile, because in all seriousness, that is how much this merger just cost. When it comes down to it, this old man just made my career. I should probably drop to my knees and suck his wrinkly old dick in thanks. On second thought, I think I just fucking vomited in my mouth.

"You have a good day, Mr. Stern. Say hello to Kay for me."

And like that, the old man walks out of the office, closing the door behind him. I listen to his footsteps making their way to the elevator as I celebrate quietly in my office. Kicking off my heels, I jump into the air with a fist pump before completing the celebration by doing the humpty dance. Tonight calls for a fucking celebration.

Sliding my pumps back on, I stroll behind my desk and pick up my phone. Thumbing through the contacts on my iPhone screen, I come to my best friend, and occasional fuck buddy, Star.

Seven and Star - what a fucking pair. Our hippy dippy parents had been friends, or more like swingers, our entire lives. I can't even tell you how many times as teenagers we found them in gross compromising positions. She has also been the only person I could rely on my entire life. Our bond goes beyond a special brand of sisterhood. The fact that we dabbled in a little muff diving together is probably the least of the issues our parents bestowed upon us.

Opening a text message, I type out the plans for the night.

Sealed the deal, bitch! See you at Sinners and Swingers at 7. We celebrate.

Tossing my cell onto the desk, I pick up the phone and dial

Olivia's extension again. This time, my bi-polar self is much nicer. I am sure the poor girl is probably scared shitless to answer her line when she sees me calling.

"Yes, Ms. James?"

"Livie, love. Can you order me one of those delish chicken wraps from that little place on the corner? You know... the one with the honey mustard." I could be speaking Russian, and she would know exactly what I needed. Which is why I pay her the big bucks.

"Sure, anything to drink?"

"Just grab me a bottle of Mountain Dew. While you are gone, stick Derek at your desk. No one else on the floor is worth a shit at taking messages. Oh, and I am out of the office for the rest of the day if anyone else calls."

I place the phone back down on the receiver, and finish up all the leftover paperwork to send down to the legal department. Such a damn load off my overflowing plate.

Sinners and Swingers isn't your typical bar. Honestly, I don't think the club would consider itself a bar at all. Most kink clubs in New York City serve alcohol, but all keep strict limits on the amount they serve to the patrons, and rightfully so.

I make my way into the club wearing a white tank top, bright red leather pants, and black stiletto heels. My long hair flows freely around my face, coming to an end somewhere around my ass. I've carefully made up my features with a hint of dark smoky makeup and my signature bright red lipstick.

Everyone here knows me; I have been a staple to this club since my twenty-first birthday. An ex-fling brought me here, hoping to interest me in a threesome. People here know me as

Mistress Marilyn, though, not as Seven.

I sit my ass down on the cheap black barstool and nod to Rex, the bartender. A smile spreads across his face as he ignores everyone else to tend to me. Flattering. He gives me a big head.

"Well, well, well! What do we have here? Mistress Marilyn, where have you been?" A seductive smile rakes across his face while he licks his lips, zeroing in on my tits.

"Oh, ya know. The real world. Gotta make that money, Rex." He nods, and ignores the others looking for booze. "Why don't you get me a shot of Jameson and a bottle of Sam Adams?"

He turns to the bar and works on my request. I turn around, eyeing the great room to see what kind of trouble I can get myself into for the night.

It has been a good month since I have had an evening to myself at Sinners and Swingers, and I want to make the most of it. Maybe I will get real lucky and have Star join me for the night. Just as my blonde BFF enters my mind, she enters the room, quickly snaking through the dancing bodies.

That is when I notice him. Evan. He is holding onto Star's hand for dear life, and she is dragging him along like a love struck puppy dog. I guess I won't be getting my fill of her perfect pink pussy tonight.

I try not to let my expression show it, but I am pissed. I hate that fucking poser, and she only likes him because of his big dick, Prince Albert and all.

"Pink this week?" I ask, referring to the Manic Panic dyed locks in her hair. It suits her, though. Perfectly.

"You like it?" she asks while she pulls me into her arms for an overly friendly hug. Her hands glide across my ass before she runs a teasing finger between my legs.

"It suits you, that is for sure." I laugh as Rex returns with my drinks. "Get Star, and *him* whatever they want. Drinks are on me tonight."

I throw back the shot of whiskey. The amber liquid burns

my throat, but damn, it hurts so good. Star wraps her arm around me, pulling me in to plant a juicy kiss on my cheek before she finally asks, “What are we celebrating tonight?”

The question of the hour. What I do in the boardroom stays there. I don't bring work home, ever. I don't bring home to work, ever. Most of my employees don't even believe I have a fucking personal life, which is pretty rich considering the life I lead when I am not in the office.

“Victory. Sweet, fucking victory, bitch!”

I grab her and plant a kiss right back on her cheek, careful not to make a play for her lips. Not only would Evan fill with rage, but I am sure Star would be pretty pissed at me for running him off.

“What third world country did you conquer this week?” Star laughs while she picks up her martini off the bar and chugs. I lift my bottle of beer to my lips and take a nice long sip, licking my lips and smiling bright enough to light up all of Manhattan.

“No country, this week. Just a name I can cross off my revenge list.” I give no more details.

“Another shot of Jameson, Rex!” I call down to the end of the bar, where the bald headed man is flirting with a dominatrix dressed in leather from head-to-toe, only her eyes peeking out from under a cat-like mask.

Many of the high society types try and hide their identity behind these doors. They hope the rest of the world will never see them for the kinky sons of bitches they really are. I’ve never thought about hiding my own identity, though; my skin and demeanor when I am here are enough to hide who I really am.

That's when he catches my eye, athough the business suit caught my eye first. As I move my eyes over his high priced clothes, I can tell he is new. That and the fact that I have never seen him here before. He turns, and I catch a pair of the most intense and beautiful blue eyes I have ever seen on a man. They shimmer like ice on a cold February day. Stubble lightly dons his strong jaw.

Although there is nothing I love more on a man that a clean haircut, and a fresh shave, his stubble looks good enough to lick.

Rex returns with my shot, and I shoot it back, followed by a chug of beer. I am done with the alcohol for the night, not that Rex would serve me much more. The club is always careful to adhere to a strict drink limit. Mixing too much alcohol with the sexual exploits of the club could become very dangerous, especially for newcomers. I'll let Star run up the tab.

She fists her martini and comes to rest beside me. “Our usual table tonight?” I nod, as she drags Evan toward the round glass table alongside the back wall.

Everything inside Sinners and Swingers is wood, deep cherry hard wood. The walls are decorated sparsely in large canvas prints, all of erotic nature. Even though it is a kink club, it is an upper class establishment, not one of those pervert filled dives where people go in hopes of scoring a blow job in the bathroom. Private suites line the side hallway and the entire second floor of the building. Places for couples or groups of consenting adults to have a little private fun. Unlike most kink clubs, Sinners and Swingers skipped the themed room bullshit. If you want an experience of that nature, this just isn't the place for you.

I start to follow Star and Evan to our usual table when I catch the mysterious new stranger staring. We make eye contact for a brief moment, and, as if there were some kind of magnetic pull, I start making my way toward him.

“I will catch up in a minute,” I whisper into Star's ear.

Is it the fact that I think he is sexy as sin, or maybe the fact that he is just fresh meat? I can't decide. What I can tell you is he never breaks my gaze as I make my way toward him.

“You’re new here,” I say to him, as a small smile hints at the corners of his lickable mouth. I extend my arm in greeting, “Mistress Marilyn, love.”

He takes my hand, and it shocks me. Like literally fucking shocks me. I haven't felt a shock like that since my older brother used to rub his feet across the funky old carpet in our Brownstone and shock me.

"Nice to meet you, Mistress Marilyn. I'm Levi." He shrugs his shoulders. Definitely a newbie or he would have been prepared with a scene name. I find him incredibly adorable, though.

"Nice to meet you Levi. Extremely nice to meet you." Poor guy; I am virtually eating him alive. "If you are up for a little fun, I will be over there with a couple friends." I motion over to Star, who is now sitting in Evan's lap. I roll my eyes at their display of public affection. Levi takes notice immediately. He chuckles to himself, and turns for the bar as I make my way back to the table.

As I sit down on the red velvet cushioned medieval looking chair, Evan whispers something into Star's ear, cuing her to grind her ass against the noticeable bulge in his much too tight skinny jeans. *Fucking God, I hate guys who wear skinny jeans. Whoever thought of making chick jeans for dudes needs to be shot.* Star leans in to me, the booze thick on her breath.

"We are gonna get outta here. This isn't really Evan's scene, plus I gotta get up early for work tomorrow." She grasps for excuses, so her boyfriend doesn't look like the total tool he is.

"Work? It's fucking eight at night. But if sissy boy can't hang, no biggie. I'm not sticking around long tonight anyway."

I'm lying. I will probably sit here 'til close, trying to muster up a little fun, even if I do have to celebrate alone.

Star stands, and I join her in goodbyes. Before I know it, her lips are on mine. I open up, ever so slightly to accept her probing tongue. Just for a moment, I get lost in her glorious mouth before she starts to pull away. I latch on to her bottom lip with a soft nibble before releasing her. Sometimes, I swear her mouth feels like home.

"Later, Star." Evan turns to me and shoots daggers in my direction, and I flip him the bird. "Sit on this, fuck bag." *God, I fucking hate him. I don't hate many people, but there is something about him that rubs me the wrong fucking way.*

And like that, I am alone. But I am used to it. I am like Pee Wee, a loner, a real rebel dotty. *Yes, I am fucking reciting Pee Wee's Big Adventure in my head. This night is going to Hell in a hand-basket.*

While I laugh at myself in my own mind, I fail to notice Levi making his way to my table. After watching him from afar, I notice the boy has done a couple laps, had a drink and hasn't caught the eye of anyone else. I'm not surprised, though; the people who come here aren't looking for the banker type. They could probably find a guy like him to fuck right at work. Typically, I wouldn't give him a second glance, either, but his eyes tell me there is something dangerous about him. I am a glutton for punishment when it comes to dangerous men.

My cell phone vibrates in my pocket, drawing my attention away from the newbie, and to my back pocket. I pull the phone out and see Star peering back at me. In the picture she set as her caller ID, she sits seductively on my bed, topless, holding her sizable breasts up with her arm, fully sleeved in My Little Pony tattoos. She takes the 80's cartoon phenomenon way too seriously.

"Hey?" I answer with curiosity, because there is no way Star should be calling me already.

"He is such a fucking douche. I am coming back."

The line goes dead and I can only wonder what the fuck transpired after they walked out. I am sure it had to do with our more than friendly parting kiss. Maybe she'll finally kick his ass to the curb. *A girl can hope!*

"Hey." Levi sits down in the chair across from me.

I turn to him. "Hey." Talk about awkward. I have to break this boy in or the others are going to eat him alive. He is so out of place, it is ridiculous.

"I have to ask you, Levi. What are you doing in a place like this?"

His eyes widen, as if he wasn't expecting the question. Someone was bound to ask him at some point, though. He leans in close, really close. Then he whispers in my ear, clearly not wanting anyone to hear whatever he is about to confess. "I have needs. Newfound kink that I need in my sex life. All the women I have been with aren't into it. So, here I am."

A look flashes on his face. I am not sure if it is embarrassment, or humiliation. Usually I am so good at reading people. I do it every day at work, but I feel bad for him. We have all been there at some point. I know I was long ago.

"It happens to the best of us, love."

I lick my bottom lip, then run my tongue across my teeth. God, he looks good enough to eat. Just as I am about to make my move, I spot Star from across the sprawling great room. "That right there is my best friend. If you play your cards right, tonight you can have us both." I wink at him as she plops her sad ass down in my lap. I can see she has been crying, and I can only wonder what that asshat said to her. She nuzzles into my neck, resting her head on my shoulder. Her blonde and neon hair curtains her face, as she continues to sniffle.

"If you'll excuse us Levi, we need a trip to the ladies' room." I throw him a smile, and he gives me a sympathetic look. He has obviously dealt with emotional women over the years; the look of understanding speaks louder than words.

Star follows close behind me, and once inside the security of the ladies' room, she finally spills her guts.

"God, he is an asshole!" she screams at the top of her lungs. If the base wasn't booming so loud through the building, I am sure the entire Upper East Side would have just heard her declaration. "He is jealous. So fucking jealous. I just can't deal with it. The second we hit the sidewalk, he picked a fight with me. It is always an issue when I am with you, Seven. It is like he thinks I am going to leave him for you!"

She huffs as she pulls a paper towel out of the steel dispenser and blots at her makeup. I let out a quiet laugh and want to help her mood desperately. "Well, I am pretty fucking sexy. And gay marriage is so legal in New York." I blow her a kiss in the mirror and she cracks a smile for me. *Mission accomplished.*

"Clearly, he just doesn't get our friendship, and if he can't accept you the way you are - the way *we* are - then fuck him. You don't need him anyways."

Throwing her bag on the counter, she pulls out a makeup bag and starts digging. She quickly fixes her face, and her mood shifts.

"I was kind of done with him anyway. Better off this way."

She shrugs, tossing the used paper products into the black garbage can and heads for the door. "Who was that guy sitting at your table?"

I wink at her, before licking my lips. "Fresh meat, my love. Fresh fucking meat."

The night goes on, and my new pet stays firmly planted at my table. I watch and socialize but eventually get bored. It's time for me to bust out of this joint for the night. I rarely ever use the private rooms at Sinners and Swingers. Not because I'm not interested, but it just isn't my thing. I would rather use my own spare bedroom. In fact, I had an entire room in my penthouse set up for exactly this type of thing. Never would I bring a hookup into my own bed.

Looking at Star, I shoot her a knowing look. Her hazy eyes tell me the only thing I need to know; the answer is yes.

"Well, Levi, this is it for us tonight. You can either come home with Star and me, or you can go home, and maybe we'll see you around sometime." He listens carefully. "But if you choose to come home with us, there are a couple rules. First, protection. Condoms are a must. I don't care how clean you are, or how clean you insist you are." He nods in agreement, and I continue my speech.

"Two. If you are afraid of strap-ons, walk away now." His eyes grow wide with lust; he's hanging on every last word. "Third, this is a one time, no strings attached kind of thing. What goes on behind those doors is private. If you take it outside those walls, I will see to it that you never step foot back inside Sinners and Swingers. Last, when we are done with you tonight, you leave. No questions asked. No phone numbers exchanged. No sleepovers. Like I said, no strings attached. Just for fun. Get it?"

He finally speaks, only to agree with everything I said.

"Got it. Clear as day, Mistress Marilyn."

He isn't nervous like so many before him have been. He is completely laid back, and I kind of admire that. I push the thoughts out of my head; this isn't a fucking love connection. This is simply fucking.

"Let's get out of here. Clyde is waiting for me anyway."

That is when the worry kicks in, all over Levi's face. He thinks we are about to throw him to a man, and he is petrified. I laugh, and reassure the poor guy. "Clyde is my driver. Relax."

His demeanor returns to laid back, and we make our way into the car, for the trip across town to my penthouse.

Clyde pulls the black Lincoln town car up in front of my John Street building in the Financial District, a bit of a drive from Sinners and Swingers. The car ride across town was quiet, even for

Star. Maybe she's lost her nerve? I wouldn't be surprised at all. Evan has really done a number on her in the month he's spent hanging around. I'm starting to doubt her devotion to the threesome in store for us.

I open the door, and step out on to the sidewalk. Star and Levi both follow me. But, as if I was reading her mind, she turns back to the car and climbs back in.

"Sorry, I'm just not feelin' it tonight, Seven. I hope you don't mind if I skip out."

I nod in her direction.

"Clyde, can you bring Star home for me please?"

He nods as the door closes. When the traffic passes, he pulls out into the streets of Manhattan like a madman.

"Well, I guess there has been a change of plans, Levi. You can go if you like. But the offer still stands."

I turn on the sidewalk, making my way through the chilly October evening to the lobby of my building. He is on my heels before I know it.

"Seven?"

I stop in my tracks. *How does he know my name? I don't want him to know my name. He needs to leave. Now.* "What did you just call me?" I turn, only to remember Star calling me by my name minutes earlier. *Fuck.*

"Look, I don't use my real name at the club. It's a privacy thing."

He nods. "I understand. If I knew better, I wouldn't have given you my real name either. But since we know each other's names now, where do we go from here?"

He moves in close, invading my space. It wasn't until now that I got a good whiff of him, and God, does he smell good. Something minty, mixed with scotch, and an expensive aftershave. Whatever that scent is, I must have it.

I meet his heated gaze, and lean further in to him, running my tongue along the stubble of his jaw. "I'm going upstairs. It is your move, Levi."

I turn away from him and enter the lobby of the building, where the warmth comforts me. Hitting the up button on the elevator, I feel an arm snake around my waist, and lips press to my ear.

"Does this mean there won't be any strap-ons tonight?"

His words send a shock through my body. This man has kink, that is for sure, and I fucking like it. Without missing a beat, I turn to face him, pressing my lips to his ear. "That all depends on what you want, Levi."

Leaving the ball in his court, I back away just in time for the elevator doors to open.

There is something about elevators. Something extremely sexy. Especially when the elevator in question has three sides of mirrors. Before I know what is happening, the door slams closed and Levi has me pinned up against the wall. His mouth moves up my neck, licking, teasing, and biting a path to my lips. He exudes control, but that is a problem, because there is no way I am letting anyone top me. He will be my bottom, or he will walk. Simple as that.

Our lips collide in a frantic explosion of need. I don't know what he wants, but I haven't been laid in some time. If I don't get a dick inside me, I may spontaneously fucking combust.

The elevator comes to a halt, signaling the end of our journey. We hit the top floor of my building, which houses my penthouse.

"We're here," I breathe into his ear as we fumble out of the elevator in each other's arms. I pull out of his embrace. I need to distance myself for a minute to set a couple things straight.

"Levi…"

He pauses and looks at me. The gorgeous blue eyes from earlier are gone; now they are dark, his pupils dilated as he watches every move I make.

"You may not have realized this in the club, and since you

are new, I will give you the benefit of the doubt." I take a few steps closer, my heels clicking loudly in the foyer, against the white tile floor, and then I closely lean in, brushing my lips against his ear. "I am not some hookup you can have your way with. In fact, it is quite the opposite, my love. You will submit to me tonight, or you will walk in that elevator, and out of my building now. Do you understand?"

Nodding his head, he slides to the floor, and kneels at my feet.

Clearly his man knows what being a submissive is all about and, holy fuck, he is turning me on. If I didn't have pants on, my cunt juices would be dripping down my leg. "Good boy."

I start toward the guest bedroom. "Come along, Levi."

The heels of my stilettos click down the short hallway, and echo through the empty space, only coming to a stop outside of the spare bedroom I use to carry on my games of sexual exploits. In here, I can be someone else. I can escape my life. I can be the slut I've ached to be since Daniel walked out on me. I could never really be myself in bed with him. Everything was just too vanilla.

Tonight is different, though; tonight is new. On most occasions, I would have Star by my side, helping to curb any personal connection to the Sub du Jour. But tonight, it will just be Levi and myself.

"Strip." I get to the point; no need for senseless chit chat. I'm not here to make friends. I am here to fuck.

I turn away from him, and slip off my heels first. Losing six inches of height, I realize Levi towers over my five foot three frame. He must have at least a foot on me. Sliding my pants down my legs, and pulling my tank top over my head, I stand in nothing but lace. My games always begin after I remove my own clothing, as the act of undressing is too intimate. Not a level of connection I choose to make with a sub on any occasion, no matter how heated we may be.

The white lace bra leaves little to the imagination. My

pierced nipples stand at attention as I steal a glimpse of the expensive suit lying crumpled on my hardwood floors. My white lace thong exposes one of the very few areas on my body not covered in ink: my luscious ass.

I slip my feet back into the stilettos, one at a time, before finally turning to examine the fine male specimen I dragged home with me this evening. I'm pleasantly surprised to see him sprawling across the bed on his back, with absolutely nothing on. Naked as the day he was born. Vulnerable to my touch.

I round the bed, side-to-side looking over every inch of his sculpted body. Clearly, he takes care of himself. I would guess the gym a couple times a week, complete with weight lifting. Mmmm… and hot damn, my favorite. Hairless from chest to ass. Freshly waxed. I would know the smooth post wax skin anywhere. Just like my own pussy.

"That suit left much to the imagination, but I can tell you, Levi…"

I crawl up on the bed, and straddle his lap before leaning in to his ear and finishing my sentence. My full breasts press against his hard chest. "I really like what I see."

I lean back on my haunches. I can feel his hardening length against my ass, and I can tell he likes everything he can see thus far. "Talk to me, Levi." I lift my leg and get off the bed, striding to the end to watch him. "Tell me what you are thinking."

His eyes stare at me, only breaking eye contact when the icy baby blues shimmy their way down my body, taking in every inch of my body.

With a low growl, he finally speaks. "I think I have died and gone to Heaven. You are perfection. Every fucking inch of your body is pure perfection."

Damn, he is going to be good for my ego. Maybe I should keep this one around? No fucking way. What the fuck am I thinking?

"I'm glad you like what you see, Levi. You're not used to

women like me. Let me guess…"

I walk over to him again, leaning onto the bed and trailing my mint green colored fingernail down the center of his stomach. "You typically go for the trophy wife type. Blonde, big fake tits, and lots of bad makeup with a side of designer clothes."

Without second thought, he nods in agreement. A slow seductive smile spreads across my face.

"I know your type all too well, Levi. You want to take a walk on the wild side, because those prissy little bitches just don't know how to fuck, right?"

I lower my mouth to his stomach, gently licking, before pressing my red lips down and sinking my teeth into him. A grunt of appreciation escapes his mouth, but he doesn't take his eyes off me. Not for a second.

"Tell me what you want, Levi. What will get you off?" Not that I really care, but knowing his turn ons will only help me draw out my own pleasure.

"Anal. Fuck me, Seven. Have your way with me."

Hearing my name roll off his tongue stops me in my tracks. Fuck. I forgot about that. But I just can't bring myself to walk away now, even though I know I probably should.

While I battle with myself, I start to eye his growing erection. It was impressive flaccid, but now that it is coming to life, it is unlike anything I have seen before. I am willing to bet, fully erect, he has to be at least a full ten inches, if not more. And the girth. Holy shit. Will that even fit?

"Stroke yourself. Jerk yourself off until you are ready to come," I demand. I am not polite, or seductive. I want to see how long his impressive length will grow.

I turn to the door, stealing my attention away from the man on my bed. I should walk away. It has already become too personal.

Reaching down between my legs, I roll my fingers across my soaked panties. It has been so long, way too long. I need a release. I need a man. I need Levi. I slide my panties down until they fall onto the floor. I step out of them, bending over without bending my knees to pick them up and giving Levi a full view of my smooth cunt. Without turning around, I know he is watching when I hear him gasp in delight.

I pick them up and toss them on the bed. I turn to watch his reaction, under my heavy lidded eyes. Without a beat, he picks them up, lifts them right to his face, and inhales deeply. *So sexy.*

"You like that?"

His attention is drawn back to my face. He is trying not to smile. So am I.

"I want to taste you." He speaks so seductively. He isn't going to have to ask me a second time. Something about him breaks down my need for control, and I give in to his want, instead of taking charge.

"I think I can arrange that. Don't stop jerking off." I am stern as I watch his hand running up and down his gorgeous cock. Each vein is noticeable. His other hand cups his balls, tugging on them. He likes pain with his pleasure. Then I remember his request from earlier. Exactly what he likes.

I open the bedroom closet, which houses all the kink toys I could ever imagine, or would personally want to use in my bedroom scenes. I reach for the lone strap-on in the closet, hiding behind the door. The black leather strap forms to my ass perfectly.

This isn't the maiden voyage with my rubber cock; in fact, I can't count the number of times I have used it on Star, or hell, the number of times she has used it on me. The thought sends a shiver down my spine and causes my clit to throb. I think I just may die if I don't get off soon. Pulling a bottle of lube off the shelf, I make my way back to my waiting plaything.

"You can stop stroking your cock now. It is time for me to play."

His gaze rakes across my body and stops when he notices my seven inch rubber dick. "Holy fuck." His eyes flash with hungry lust. "You are a fucking goddess." He licks his lips and raises up on his elbows. His words cause my stomach to churn.

"Don't get any thoughts just yet. First, you are going to lick my cunt until I come all over your face. Then I will think about fucking you - depending on your performance. The better you do, the harder I will fuck you. Deal?"

I unstrap the fake dick and crawl up his body. His arm snakes around my back to unclasp the bra I left on. Such a brazen boy for someone who should be submitting to me, but it sparks something deep inside of me. Is it desire? I push the warning bells into the back of my mind, where they will stay until I am done fucking for the night.

His lips crash against mine in an urgent dance of need. I part my mouth, snaking my tongue into his so I can explore that perfect mouth before it explores my drenched cunt. His dick is rock hard between our meshing bodies.

We continue to feast on each other's mouths, and then he moves suddenly. I am on my back, pressed against the bed, with his lean body hanging above me. His mouth breaks away from mine, but only to trail his tongue south. Every inch his mouth covers, my body flames with need.

Stopping at my breasts, he pays extra special attention to each barbell-clad nipple, teasing and tugging on them. I let a moan escape from my mouth, which further encourages him. *Fuck, his mouth is good.* In one final movement, his tongue trails over my tattooed stomach and dives right between my aching folds.

"What I wouldn't do to trace every single line of these tattoos with my tongue."

His words take me off guard, but without missing a beat, he is lapping up my sweet cream and nibbling on my pearl. He is a master with his mouth, sucking and lapping like he is enjoying an ice cream cone. In no time flat, I can feel myself teetering on the brink of explosion. Parting my pussy lips, he runs his skilled tongue in and out, fucking me with his mouth. Gentle flicks of his hot tongue tease my hard nub. He is barely making contact, but driving me wild.

I claw at the duvet on the bed and dig the heels of my stilettos into the mattress. With one last suck on my clit, I explode. "Oh FUCK! Fuck. Fuck. Holy. Oh. My. God. FUCK!" I am loud enough to wake the dead, but it has been an eternity since I have had someone go down on me with that kind of skill. My body is covered in a thin sheen of sweat, and my chest heaves like I ran a marathon.

Looking down between my legs, I can see the look of satisfaction on his face, which is covered in my juices. Now it is my turn to give him exactly what he wants.

"Good boy," I praise him. "You ready to get fucked?"

My legs feel like Jell-O, but I manage to get off the bed, and strap my fake cock back on.

"More than you fucking know," he says while licking my orgasm off his lips.

"Bend over, feet on the floor, and lean on the bed."

Without hesitation, he follows my orders. I grab the bottle of lube off the bed and squirt it all over the plastic dick, coating it completely. With Levi in place, I lick up his spine, sending a shiver through his waiting body. Parting his ass cheeks, I squirt more lube onto his waiting hole, and position the tip at his back door. Instead of tensing up, his body relaxes with ease, unlike any man I have ever seen get into this kind of kink. He is a pro; he expects every delicious little movement I will give him.

"You ready, Levi?"

He grunts, and I push in slowly. His strong arms fist the bed sheets as I make my initial entrance. With little effort, my dildo slips right in. This is not the first time he has done this.

"You like that?" I croon to him. He takes a deep breath as the cock bottoms out in his ass before finally replying to me.

"I never thought it could be this good. Doing it by myself will never be the same again." He grunts again, followed by a sultry moan.

I apply a bit more lube, pulling out and massaging it in before I slam back into him. The sensations of the strap-on rubbing on my clit is fantastic. Priming my body for another orgasm. I pump into his ass quickly, trying to stay steady on my feet in these six inch heels. The only way I could fuck him was by leaving them on. But damn, if this isn't hot I don't know what is.

I reach around, taking his cock in my hand, stroking it to meet my thrusts from behind. His deep moans turn into growls while I continue pumping his cock and ass in an urgent rhythm.

"FUCK!" he screams, and I can feel the cum shooting out of his dick, right onto my heels. "Oh SHIT! Fuck! Seven! Holy! You. Are. A. Fucking. God. Don't stop. Don't fucking stop. Pump my ass baby. Harder!"

His screams of ecstasy ring through the room, and I give him exactly what he wants. Grabbing both of his hips, I slam into him from behind as he continues to empty his orgasm onto my feet.

"You were a good boy, Levi. But now, you need to lick all that come off my shoes, and then you are going to fuck me. I want to take that big cock for a ride."

I pull my dick out of his ass, and unstrap it, letting it fall to the floor with a thud. I stay in place, waiting for my directions to be followed. He falls to his knees on the floor and starts to lick his release off my stilettos.

Nothing is more erotic than watching a man lick his own come off my feet. Maybe it is a kink of mine, but holy hell. I am ready to mount that gorgeous beast of a cock and ride it like Seabiscuit.

He licks the last teardrop of seed off my foot and I step out of the stilettos. "Climb up on the bed and stroke yourself hard for me. It is my turn."

Without, hesitation he has his fist around his dick, jerking as if his life depended on it.

It doesn't take him long at all before his cock is standing at attention for me. Picking up a foil packet out of the nightstand drawer, I wonder if the condom is even going to roll down his long length. But it will have to do.

I rip the packet open with my teeth, crawling back onto the bed. I take his beautiful dick in my mouth for one nice long deep throat. I open wide to accommodate the thickness, only making it half way down his shaft before it bumps the back of my throat. I slowly roll the latex down his throbbing erection. Perfection, absolute perfection, in the form of a dick.

"You ready?" I ask, moving up his body and resting my dripping pussy right on his toned abs.

"Oh, I am more than ready. I've been waiting to get that little cunt around my dick all night."

God, I love it when guys talk dirty. His words vibrate all the way into my womb. I move back just a bit, and he guides his thick cock into my primed cunt.

"Oh, fuck. You are big."

Big isn't even the word for it. I can feel him everywhere as I slowly slide down his dick. I can feel every wall in my tiny cunt stretching to take his monster of a dick. It is the biggest cock I have ever had the pleasure of breaking me in two.

But damn, it feels good. I slowly start to rock my hips, while I continue adjusting to his size. My warm, tight folds ache as they stretch with the pleasure of his cock.

"You have the tightest pussy I have ever had the pleasure to fuck."

His words bring out the wild woman in me. I lift my ass and slam it back down as my juices flow, coating his beautiful, throbbing erection with each thrust. I pace myself, slowly rocking, rubbing my swollen nub against him over and over again. I can't help but pant like a dog in heat.

My body lets go and the moans flow like water. His grunts and growls match each noise I make. The head of his dick finds my g-spot and I throw my head back in pleasure. “Oh, yes! Right there, big boy,” I gasp out in between gasps for air. With each thrust I can feel my aching pussy stretching to accommodate his thick shaft. Deeper and harder as his balls slap on my ass, as his length bottoms out, slamming into my womb. I am in heaven.

He grunts into my ear as he runs his tongue along my neck, sucking and biting along the way. “Fuck, Seven. You have the tightest cunt I have ever fucked. Mmmmmmm. God, I fucking love it.”

He raises his ass to meet each of my thrusts. His dick pushes deeper when I didn't think it could go any further. “Oh yeah, ride that dick, baby.”

“Oh God!” I cry out while I grind down onto him. His dick presses on my sweet spot as he runs his thumb over my swollen clit. “Oh yeah. Fuck. That's it. Right there,” I call out as I slam down onto his cock again.

“Fuck that dick, baby; fuck it hard,” he whispers into my ear, before taking my budded nipple into his mouth. I explode in a blinding orgasm. I scream and shout all kinds of curses, mixed with pure animalistic sounds. My pussy contracts in pleasure as the world crashes down around me. I claw my nails down his chest as I continue my frantic pace, drawing out the pleasure. I am incoherent, but he continues the rhythm without missing a beat. One, two, three pumps, and I can feel his dick twitching, as my cunt continues to milk him dry with the aftershocks of probably the best orgasm of my life.

Exhausted, I fall onto his chest. His dick is still deep inside me. I literally could fall asleep, just like this. But I know I have to send him on his way into the night. Fuck. I don't want to; he would make such a fun plaything. Damn me for having rules when it comes to fucking.

“Okay, big boy. Time for you to get dressed.”

I pull his dick out of my satisfied cunt, and head for the closet once more. I grab the pink robe hanging from a hook on the door and throw it on.

"You were serious? This really is a one time thing?" The surprise in his voice actually catches me off guard. I explained it before we even got to my penthouse. One. Time. Thing.

"Of course I was serious. As much as I enjoyed our evening, there won't be a repeat performance. But Levi, thank you."

I wink at him and throw the ball of his clothes onto the bed. He gets the message and begins to dress.

"You know your way out."

As I walk out the door, I give him a wave and disappear to the other side of the penthouse.

CHAPTER 2

Friday Morning

Instead of driving to my office this morning, Clyde makes his way across town to the Alexander Mobile headquarters on Park Ave. The streets are bustling with businessmen making their way to their offices, which are scattered all over the city that never sleeps. Taxis swerve in and out of traffic like kamikazes on a mission.

The car comes to a stop. I grab my laptop case, and exit. Setting my black Jimmy Choo pumps onto the sidewalk, I run my hands down the white skirt that falls just above my knee, over the black thigh high stockings that match the long sleeve black and white polka dot top under my peacoat, and I walk into Alexander Mobile like I own the place. Well, I kind of do now; at least, my company does.

I pause briefly at the security desk to grab my badge and become more acquainted with the security staff. I'll be setting up an office in the building, so everyone is going to become quickly familiar with me. As I take strong, sure strides to the elevator, I observe strangers staring, while exchanging whispers. The rumor mill has been rich in the wake of Mr. Stern's shares being sold, but I don't think anyone expected my powerhouse ass to be taking his spot.

It's nine-fifteen, and I'm banking on the board of directors being in the meeting room as planned. Being on time is not negotiable for me, ever. It is one of my biggest pet peeves. I don't need directions, and I hop in the elevator for the thirty-fourth floor. I've been in this office a number of times over the past month, securing the deal of a lifetime. I could navigate this space with my eyes closed.

The doors open and close. People come and go. Finally, after what seems like the longest elevator ride of my life, the doors open to the sprawling executive offices of Alexander Mobile. With a determined step, I walk toward the glass-sided conference room. Mr. Stern catches my glance and meets me at the door with open arms. I place a chaste kiss on his cheek and enter the room.

The men at the table fall silent. All stares turn toward me, just as Mr. Stern sits down in the luxurious office chair next to me.

"Board members, I would like you to meet your new boss. This is Ms. James."

Without looking at the men, I place my laptop case down on the table. "Good morning, gentlemen. It is nice to meet you all. Why don't you all take a moment and introduce yourselves? Starting with you." I point to the large, balding man to my left, pulling my laptop out, and setting up my makeshift work station at the head of the table. I take off my coat as the men start to sound off like a prison roll call.

"Edward Williams."

"Jonathan Stein."

"Matthew Sullivan."

"Daniel Alexander."

"How nice to see you again, Daniel. We'll have to catch up." I wave on the next guy, not giving Daniel any more attention. He's completely stunned.

"Aaron O'Donnell."

"Levi Parker."

His voice, his name. I look up, across the sprawling dark wood table, and make eye contact with the last voice. Levi Parker. Holy. Fucking. Shit. My heart skips a beat, and I see my career falling apart before my eyes. The guy I fucked two nights ago, up the goddamn ass with a strap-on, is one of my new fucking board members. I. Am. So. Fucked. *So* fucked. So beyond fucked.

My nerves are on fire, and I do everything I can not to flip the fuck out in front of these men who should be fearing me. Daniel's attention is piqued as Levi and I exchange glances across the table.

Calm the fuck down, Seven. Calm down.

I hit Daniel with a smile, and start my business as if I didn't just have an internal mental breakdown.

"Good morning, gentlemen. It is nice to meet you all. Please give me a couple days to become acquainted with everyone. Your names will be my first priority. I am sure Mr. Stern has filled you in on all the details of the purchase of Alexander Mobile."

The men nod, and continue to watch me like a hawk. "There will be a series of changes over the next few weeks. I will be bringing in a five person team to audit the way business is handled. As you know, this is typical protocol with any corporate takeover. I will also be setting up an office here, where Mr. Stern currently houses his, since today is the last day he will be with us. I will be here two full days a week, Wednesday and Friday, and two half days a week. Monday morning, and Thursday morning." I pull out a stack of business cards, and start walking the room, stopping at each man to pass one along. "All of my contact information is available on these cards. Email is the easiest way to contact me, but my cellphone, and office line at White-Woods Global are listed. Do not hesitate to use them if needed." I pause in front of Levi as I hand the card over.

He doesn't make eye contact. He barely acknowledges the

card. Maybe he's as nervous as I am about this entire thing. Maybe, just maybe, he will forget the night ever happened. Wishful thinking? Yes. Reality? Probably not. If he enjoyed it half as much as I did, he has been dreaming about it every night since. I've fucked a lot of guys in my day, but there was just something about the encounter as a whole; I just can't shake it.

"If there isn't anything pressing, I am going to show myself to Mr. Stern's office. I will be available until noon today. Please, don't hesitate to stop in." I close my laptop, slip it into my bag, grab my jacket off the back of the chair, and hightail it the fuck out of there. Never looking back to see the kind of looks floating around the conference room. Men like them don't like a woman in charge. They don't want to answer to a woman at work. Which is why I am a rarity in the boardroom.

I find my way into Mr. Stern's office, and it has already been cleaned out. He sits on the sofa in the corner, sipping on a glass of single malt Scotch. *Jesus, old man, it's not even noon.*

"Make yourself at home, Seven."

I place my bag down on the desk, and he rises to his feet. "I was just on my out anyway. I have to make my rounds through the departments. Say my goodbyes." Like that, the old man walks out without a second thought. *Whatever.*

Pulling out my laptop, I take on my biggest task of the day: my email inbox. What a fucking nightmare, as always. Typing away, distracted by the internet, I hear the door open. Automatically assuming Mr. Stern forgot something, I ignore whoever enters the room. It isn't until I can feel a set of eyes burning a hole into me that I look up from my busy work.

Levi is standing at the desk, his cold blue eyes burning holes through me. He doesn't speak, and we spend a long moment engaging in a staring competition. Something I outgrew about ten years ago. I break the silence. "Levi."

"Seven." He returns the uncomfortable formality between us.

“What can I help you with?” I try to break the tension, but I already know why he’s in my office.

“I think we should talk. You know. About, well...” He stops, because he is as uncomfortable as I am with the situation.

“Look, had I known we would be in this position, I would never have offered the other night. But since we’ve found ourselves in this precarious situation, I’d rather not talk about it now, or inside these office walls. We can meet up after work, but this conversation isn't happening here.”

He nods in agreement.

“Tonight, we'll do dinner.” He speaks with certainty. I don't want to like his demand, but I cave to the offer.

I nod in his direction. “Seven at Tokyo Fusion on 34th,” I say before shrugging him off. He nods and walks out of the office, just as Daniel decides to enter. *Seriously, this is turning out to be the most complicated fucking buyout ever.*

“Seven James. I can honestly say, I never thought I would see you again.” His words slice through me like a knife. Something about him is like pouring salt in the wounds of my raw soul. I should be overjoyed to be here, taking the only job he has ever wanted, but seeing him face-to-face still fucks with my mind on so many different levels. Age hasn't been kind to him. His previously thick sandy blonde hair is thinning, and a bald spot peers through. You can tell he’s desperately tried to cover it. I chuckle to myself. Wrinkles surround his eyes, and worry lines are front and center. If I didn't know any better, I dodged a bullet when he walked out on me. *Ugly ass!*

“Daniel Alexander. We meet again, love.” I smile, and stand. As I brush my skirt down, I’m sure to accent every curve he’s missing out on. “It has been ages, what... seven years?” I know it’s been five, but adding time helps.

“Five, only five,” he replies as a smile begins to pull at the corner of his mouth. Slow and seductive. The same smile he used to win me over, so many years ago.

"Five, huh? Well, it really is a pleasure to see you. You look..." I want to say horrible, but I keep it polite. Kill 'em with kindness, right? "Great. You look great Daniel." I extend my arms, and give him a big, friendly bear hug.

"I have to admit, I never thought I'd see you in a boardroom, let alone mine." He speaks with confidence, like he actually has ownership in this company.

"Actually, it is your father's boardroom, but continue." The little dig makes me feel so much better.

"How have you been? Are you married? Please, let's catch up." He sits down, and I walk around the desk, plopping down in my chair. My eyes drag over his left hand, wedding band firmly in place on his ring finger, and I know the answer to so many of my questions already.

"Single as the day I was born. I don't need a pesky romance in the way of my plans to conquer the world." I laugh at my own joke, as does Daniel. He knows me well enough to know it really isn't a joke at all. "Just been busting my ass, living the young, wild, and free lifestyle. I can see you settled down. What was her name? Susan? Sheryl? Sidney?"

With barely a smile, he corrects me. "Samantha." Samantha Rockwell. I knew her well enough, but wouldn't give him the pleasure of that slice of knowledge.

"Just darling. Any children?" He always wanted a big brood of brats. Kids, just not my thing.

"Three, actually. We have twin girls who just turned one, and a six week old little boy."

I have to laugh; that's a shitload of kids in a year.

"Wow. Well, they must keep you busy." I silently laugh at the miserable, sleep-deprived look on his face. The admission of that flock just explains part of the reasons why he looks like he's been rode hard, and put up wet. "They must be a handful!"

"Oh, that is an understatement. Samantha really has her hands full." I could imagine. No. Not really. Nor would I ever want to image.

"Well, Daniel, it was great catching up, but I have a ton of emails I need to sift through before I leave here at noon. I'll be back on Monday morning. If you need anything in between now and then, feel free to shoot me an email." I smile; it's fake, and I hope he can't see through the show.

"I look forward to working with you, Seven." Like that, he is gone.

I came here to take his job from him, take the company he thought would be handed over to him when his father retired, had the fool not lost the majority of his stocks to Mr. Stern a decade ago. However, the bold man I once knew is gone, replaced by the shell of a broken man. I thought I would get a thrill from this deal, but in reality, I only feel bad for him. All those years of plotting revenge down the shitter. He ran his own life into the ground without any help from me.

I pick up the phone and dial Olivia. On the first ring, her cheerful voice greets me.

"Livie, get me Mikal, my interior decorator. I want this office overhauled by the time I get back on Monday."

My phone vibrates across the sprawling antique oak desk, signaling a message. Without looking, I know it's Star. She doesn't like to talk on the phone; text is her preferred method of communication. It's been two full days since the blow out with Evan, and she completely went off the radar. It's her coping method, so I always just leave her be.

Star: 1 Evan: 0 I am done with him completely. How

was your night with Mr. Fresh Meat?

I let out a sigh, thinking about the night I shared with Levi; it was off the charts. Something I would more than enjoy doing on a regular basis. But just like every other hookup in life, it's in the past now. Exactly where it would stay, unfortunately. An unfamiliar twinge of emotion rips through my stomach. *What the fuck do you call that?*

It was hot. Off the fucking charts. Fucked him six ways to Sunday and sent him on his merry way. But, it's fucking complicated now. Really fucking complicated.

As much as I'm not the kind of girl to spill my problems to a room full of BFF's after a slumber party with manis and pedis, Star is my other half, my built-in therapist in life. I can tell her anything, just like she can do the same. In time, we would sit down to have drinks and she would spill the details of her relationship with Evan. From the sex, all the way to the breakup. It's like a form of therapy for her too. As far back as we could remember, we both had each other, and really no one else. Well, I do have an older brother, but I haven't seen him in ages.

The phone vibrates again.

Complicated like how? You're not going to see him again right?

I spit out the Starbucks tea I'm sipping on, spraying my computer screen with the faded pink liquid. Again? What the fuck is that?

That is the problem, I will. Walked into my new boardroom at Alexander Mobile this morning. He is a fucking board member here. I have to work with him.

Daily. FML!

The humor of the situation would give her a laugh. I'm sure she's sitting on the other end of the phone hooting over my own misfortune. Out of all the hookups in my life, and fucking believe me, there have been plenty, something like this has never happened. Ever. Work and play have never crossed paths, and honestly, I never thought I'd see the day when they did.

It would all have to wait, sit on the back-burner until dinner tonight, when I would sit down as a businesswoman and discuss the arrangements we would have to live by from here on out. I can deal with Levi; he seems like a pleasant enough guy. I'm positive he won't want our rendezvous to be boardroom knowledge; it would mar his reputation far more than mine. In fact, I can use that leverage to my benefit. He keeps his mouth shut; if not it will be the funeral of his career, not mine.

You have got to be kidding me, right? Board member! Well, if he was good in the sack, why not just go for an office affair? He married?

Married? I doubt it. But knowing all the other board members donned wedding bands, including Daniel, it only makes me think he has something to hide. *What the fuck? Why do I care about his current relationship status? Jesus!* I need to clear my head, leave for the damn day already.

I won't be carrying on an office affair, it's in the past. One time. No strings. You know how I roll.

It was the truth. Not since Daniel, the man who took my virginity, did I sleep with the same man, or woman, twice. Only Star.

Looking over at the clock, it finally reads six. I'd only

expected to stay at the Alexander Mobile building half a day, but stacks of paperwork kept me swamped with business. An hour is all I have to get home, change, and make my way to dinner, where I will start my game of blackmail with Levi. Although I hope it doesn't come to that.

CHAPTER 3

Dinner

I didn't have time to stop at home and change, so I wear the same skirt and polka dot top that I wore to work earlier in the day. The host of Tokyo Fusion and I are on a first name basis. Vee takes me back to my table, and I order sake and some fancy Japanese beer. The need to unwind after a long day in the office is greater than I'd originally anticipated. On a typical Friday night, I would be soaking in my garden tub, listening to Skillet before heading to Sinners & Swingers and looking for some action. But tonight, I am forced to clean up a mess. A really big mess that *I* made, for once.

I sip on my beer, keeping my eye on the front door while I scroll through email messages, figuring out what's urgent, and what can be put off until Monday morning. My email inbox always will be the bane of my existence.

Absorbed in an email from my mother, I completely miss Levi walking through the door. His presence goes unnoticed until he's standing in front the table.

"Seven?" His voice rings through my entire body, sending goosebumps across my flesh. Not exactly the kind of reaction I was anticipating by any means.

"Have a seat." I motion to the other side of the intimate booth I requested, tucked away in the back corner. Instead, he plants himself down next to me, his thigh grazing the bare skin peeking out from under my skirt. It's only then I notice the strap of my black garter belt, which is visible. *Fuck.*

"I don't want to make this any more difficult than it has to be. We clearly have to work together and I would hate for the one night we shared to get in the way of our careers." My words are precise and to the point. No beating around the bush, because that simply isn't me.

"Seven, when you walked into that boardroom this morning, my entire world shattered into a thousand pieces." He runs his left hand through his messy brown hair, and lets out a deep breath. "The other night. God. I haven't been able to stop thinking about it. I was tempted to find you. I Googled you. I wanted to leave a note for you at your front desk. But I didn't want to come across like a fucking stalker." His words hit me like he just punched me in the face. Seriously, I may have preferred being punched over continuing whereever this conversation was headed.

"Yeah, stalker skills don't get any points from me." I try to lighten the mood, but his blue eyes are no longer icy. They are as hot as fire, flaming with something. Lust, maybe?

"I've never been connected with someone like that. On that level." His words sent a shock through my system. Who the fuck is this guy, and why does he seem to have some deeper impact on me? *Not fucking cool; not cool at all.*

"Wait. Please. Before you go on, Levi. It wasn't a connection; it was just sex. That's all. Really *great* sex." I hold my hand up in defense, trying to put another inch of space between us.

I'm cornered against the wall as he moves in closer. "You thought it was really great sex too?" His face lights up as he speaks. I gave myself away. He's keen, smart, a receptive man, and he picked up on my words the moment they fell out of my mouth.

"Of course, it was hot. You can't make a girl like me come a couple times without knowing it was some damn good sex. But Levi, that is all it was. There was no magical connection. If anything, it was a sexual connection. Something I've had in the past. There is a lot more to me than meets the eye." It was the truth; well, sort of. Yeah, I've had great sex over the years. But I would never tell him that our night ranked up there with the time I fucked Adam Levine in the dressing room at Radio City.

He moves in closer and closer. I have nowhere else to go. I'm pinned against the wall and he is blocking the only exit. His thigh grazes mine. "Come home with me, Seven." His words caress my body with need, as his breath heats my neck. They promised every pleasure I know he could fulfill. I want so badly to say yes. Not because I like him, but because I can feel my clit swelling with need simply from talking about riding his beautiful dick again.

"I don't think that would be a good idea, Levi." My words are short, but my voice cracks as I speak them. He knows I'm lying. I think it would be a fucking fantastic idea, but the boss in me knows that, with all the office fraternization policies I've put into place, it is a horrible idea.

"I think it would be a fantastic idea. No one would ever have to know." He pauses only for a moment to lick the sensitive spot right behind my ear. I melt against his body, as he presses me up against the wall. "It can be our secret. We keep on working together, and all the while, I get the pleasure of knowing I am fucking the boss. Or better yet. The boss is fucking me. Up. The. Ass."

A shiver runs down my spine, and I am over the idea of dinner. The only thing I am hungry for is him. The waitress comes over to take our order, and I snap back to reality very quickly. *What the fuck was I thinking?*

"I'll have my usual." She quickly notes down my orange chicken over white rice, with extra sauce, then turns her glare to

Levi, who clearly hasn't considered what was on the menu, other than me. "I'll have beef and broccoli. Heavy on the broccoli, with a Coke."

He waves her off, and focuses his attention back on me. Those eyes… I swear he can see straight through me, which scares the ever living shit out of me. One thing I have always prided myself on is hiding my emotions like a pro. My fucked up childhood ensured I would be a gold medalist in the emotionally void category. But this man acts like he can read my soul.

"I can't. I'm sorry Levi. As much as I would like to - and believe me, I would *really* like to- I just can't."

I can see the rage building within him. He is mad, like really mad. Slowly he pushes away from me, and my body starts to ache for his touch again. Fucking traitor. He turns away before sliding out. *Is he really going to leave after he just ordered dinner? That would be rude!* Instead of walking for the exit, though, he slides into the booth bench across the table from me. His look is guarded, and his lips are pressed together tightly. He looks like a businessman sitting down to command a deal, and I am completely thrown off my game.

"You know, Seven. I came here giving you the benefit of the doubt."

What? Okay, so now he has my fucking attention; if he thinks he is going to get any kind of upper hand on me, he is sadly mistaken. He takes a sip from the glass of ice water placed in front of me on the table, savoring the cold, wet liquid, while never taking his eyes off mine.

"When there is something I want, I get it. And I want you. I want you all the time. I want what we had Wednesday night. I want more. And I *will* get it."

Is this guy for real? My temper is brewing. I'm a ticking time bomb, which is about to blow up in what could possibly be a very public meltdown.

"You. Listen. To. Me. Levi." My words half resemble a

growl. "You will not push me. You will not threaten me. I don't know *who* you think I am, but I will ruin you." I take a sip of my beer, and gather myself together to shoot him a smile. Fake and dazzling. The calm before the storm I am about to unleash.

"I came here with the intentions of being nice, civil, even friendly. People don't get friendly from me, *especially* when I am their boss. But I gave you the benefit of the doubt, because I fucking like you, Levi Parker. But do not mistake my kindness for weakness, because we all know I am the one in charge here. In the boardroom and the bedroom. Don't think for one second that I didn't notice your need for submission under my hand."

I run my tongue along my bottom lip as my eyes take in the rest of his body, taking in his mannerisms and the change in his body language. A moment ago he took me on with bravado; now he is ready to cower like a lamb. "I make the rules - here, in the boardroom, and in the bedroom. And if you want to get back in my good graces, you better fucking wow me."

A sly smile spreads across his face; he thinks he has won. But little does he know there is no way I am going to let him back into my bed. I made that decision the night he walked out of my penthouse. The knowledge of working together is just icing on the cake now.

"So, why don't we take this time to get to know each other a bit, Seven?"

The floor is pulled out from under me. *Know* me? What is this, the fucking *Love Connection*?

Maybe I will play the game, pull what I want to know out of him, maybe gather a little intel on Alexander Mobile, and Daniel. Good idea.

"What is it you want to know, Levi?" I wave my hand at him. "I'm an open book." If he only knew.

His teeth tug on his bottom lip, and he runs his tongue across his top teeth. "Are you single, Seven?" Question of the hour. Does he really want to know me, or just size me up?

"Yes, have been for years. Although I am married to my work. Yourself?" I'm willing to bet he has a hot little Stepford wife, just like Daniel does. These New York City business types all do.

"Single. Divorced actually. My wife left me about two years ago."

Interesting. Submissive little Levi was left by his wife, but I am sure there is more to the story. "Kids?" I question with confidence.

"None. Couldn't have any. Part of the reason she left me. I couldn't provide her with what she wanted out of life, so she found it with my partner at the firm I was working at."

Yikes, that is harsh. I feel like I should apologize to him for that. "Damn, sorry I asked."

His face shows relief, instead of pain. "She did me a favor. I didn't want kids anyway. I am not really the parent type." He shrugs his shoulders as the waitress arrives with our food.

We eat and talk, discussing all the mundane details of life. Our night reminds me a lot of time I would spend with Star. The conversation comes easily; nothing is off topic, but we don't push to know the deep dark secrets we are both clearly hiding. I like to consider myself pretty damn good at reading strangers. If I didn't know any better, he was hiding something just as deep and dark as I, under the layers of our public personas.

A dinner I'd anticipated to take an hour and a half at most flows into three hours. We clear our plates, even sharing a few bites here and there. I indulge in a few more beers than I probably should, but I don't have anything to do in the morning, so what do I care? But the best part of the entire evening comes in the form of deep fried ice cream. The out of this world vanilla treat is probably my favorite at Tokyo Fusion. I laugh to myself as I lick the vanilla ice cream off the spoon. *Vanilla, what a fucking joke. My life is beyond fucked up, and my favorite flavor in the world is vanilla.*

The check comes, and he picks up the tab like a gentleman.

I have to give him the slightest bit of credit for that.

"I had a nice time this evening. Once you got your head out of your ass and stopped trying to threaten me, that is." I laugh, while I pull my purse out from under the table and scoot across the booth for the exit.

"I did, too. I'm sorry about the threat. Truly. I'm just not used to being told no, Seven. I didn't know what to do." He is embarrassed; it is kind of adorable. *Adorable? What the fuck? He isn't a puppy, Seven; get your shit together.*

As I stand, I lose my balance, totally blaming the last shot of sake. "Damn it!" But before I can land on my ass in the packed eatery, a strong arm loops around my waist, saving the day. Or at least my ass from a huge purple bruise in the morning.

"Sorry about that." He pulls his arm free and takes a step back, desperate to put a sizable distance between our electrifying connection. Any time a single hair on my body comes in contact with him, I feel something only those bimbos in romance novels drag on about. Romance is for old housewives and desperate twats.

I come to reality, realizing that Levi is still staring at me, and I'm lost somewhere in my brain. I clearly took a wrong turn at the frontal lobe and got lost somewhere in the sensory cortex.

"It's okay. Thanks for saving my ass. Literally." I laugh, as I let my guard down just a smidge. It's an involuntary response. Maybe it's the alcohol, or maybe it is just the fact that, for the first time since Daniel, I have enjoyed the company of a man in a social setting. Not just in my bed.

"I wouldn't want to see that pretty ass hurt." His words throw me off. Here I was giving him the benefit of the doubt. I thought he'd let the pursuit go. *Silly Seven*!

"Not going to work, Mr. Parker." I throw him a side eye, and walk for the doors.

It's a chilly night in the city, but I can't help but want to walk. Sometimes the beauty of the skyscrapers and neon lights do it for me. Give me three blocks, of course, and I'll be calling Clyde to pick my ass up because my feet feel like they are about to fall off.

Looking up in the sky, I can actually see stars, which is pretty rare in this neck of the woods, and I am determined to use the view for clarity. Until I realize Levi is behind me, following me.

I turn to him. "I had a nice evening, but this is where it ends." I extend my arm to shake his hand, because that is as close as I am going to let him get. There is no way I am going to opt for a hug, even if it is one of those half hugs dudes exchange. His eyebrow lifts, as he lets out a chuckle. *Is he laughing at me? Fucker.*

"It was a nice night, I agree. But it would be even nicer if you came home with me, Seven."

Nope. No way. No how. Not happening. "I'm sorry, Levi. You just know I can't. It's not you. I had a great time tonight. I just can't."

His hand takes mine, finally giving in to the only kind of friendly contact he is going to get from me, and I can feel the lust swimming through my blood. My body screams want, while my brain screams reason. No man, not even Daniel, has ever had this kind of hold on me. I smile while releasing his grip and turn to walk away. A couple yards down the sidewalk, I can hear his feet stomping heavily. He's running in my direction. Why couldn't he just have walked in the other direction?

"Seven! Wait." Like a flash, he is by my side, panting. "Tomorrow night, have dinner with me again."

I run my hand through my hair, trying to compose myself before I speak. Instantly an evil yet genius plan strikes me, a sure way to get him to lose interest. "Dinner, no. My Saturday nights are spent at Sinners & Swingers. But you may join me there for the night, if you dare. Ten sharp."

My legs carry me away as quickly as the Jimmy Choos will allow, and I pull my cellphone out of my purse to dial Clyde. I won't be getting a clarity walk tonight, but I won't need it. My plan was genius enough to send Levi running for the hills. And get me off on top of it.

Corset? Check.
Crotchless panties? Check.
Vibrator? Check.
Condoms? Check.

I was ready to rock ‘n' roll for the night, but instead of the show taking place inside my spare bedroom, I’m finally going to break down and utilize a private room at the club. There will be no offers of coming back to my place; I’m going to make sure of that.

I zip up my knee high red leather boots and bend over in front of the mirror to see exactly how much of my ass can be seen when I do. *Just enough.*

Clyde is waiting downstairs. I throw on my knee length, black coat and hit the elevator. Tonight will make or break everything with Levi. I can’t let him continue to pursue me; it’s just not in the cards. Everything about my life is on a detailed plan, which he does not fit into. Only in my boardroom, and if I was really a shitty person, he would be gone from there already. I gave him the benefit of the doubt, for sure.

The ride from my penthouse to the club is peaceful, but I have far too much time inside my own head trying to analyze everything. My emotions. My physical response to him. My lack of concern for his feelings, kind of. The reasons why I will never let another person get close to me. The reasons why I’ve only ever found myself emotionally connected to Star, after what the devastation Daniel had put me through. After I had finally opened up.

Star sat next to me on a worn mattress, in the back of an old Volkswagen bus, somewhere in upstate New York. It was cold, really fucking cold for a September night, and our parents were nowhere to be found, again. We huddled together trying to stay warm under the lone afghan that had been left behind. Sharing a pillow, we wrapped our arms around each other in an attempt to share body heat for warmth. Her voluptuous breasts pressed through the thin material of her t-shirt, up against my stomach. I could feel her pebbled nipples, and the only thought in my mind was how they would taste. Not how we could stay warm.

Her hand gently brushed my back. Up and down. Trailing her finger along my spine in an intimate motion. Her warm breath caressed my neck, as she moved in closer, and closer until her lips met my collarbone. Goosebumps spread across my skin. Internally, I tried to blame it on the cold, but I knew it was her touch bringing me to life.

"Star," I whispered. Her pale face and hazel eyes looked up, pleading with me not to stop what she was doing. Without a second thought, I leaned in and kissed her. My tongue brushed her bottom lip, as she moved up my body with need.

Her soft lips parted, and my tongue slipped in to explore her mouth. It tasted like cherries; maybe it was just her lip gloss but it was heaven. My body acted on instinct, moving up and cupping her full breasts. I ran my finger over her nipple and she moaned loudly into my mouth. Not trying to cover up the pleasure my touch brought. Her whimpers were enough to encourage me under the shirt.

Her breasts hung free, without the protection of a bra. I wanted to taste them. I wanted to suck on her nipples like an infant feasting on its mother. The intimate encounter had my pussy soaking through my panties and thin sweatpants. Her knee moved between my legs, nestling right on my sweet spot, and I let out a long moan of my own.

Star pinned me under her touch, and I pushed her shirt up as she hung over me. Her breasts dangled in my face. I lifted my head off the pillow and took the tiny pink bud into my mouth, sucking it as if my life depended on it. Her moans cheered me on, as I licked tenderly with my tongue.

"Oh yeah. Seven, that feels so good." My first taste of sexual contact with a woman. My first taste of dirty talk, and it drove me crazy. I moved to taste her other breast and she threw her head back in ecstasy. She loved my touch. Moving my hands south and becoming brazen, I slid them inside the matching pair of thin sweatpants she wore. Over a thin mound of hair, I ran my middle finger through her wet folds. Her pussy is as wet as mine.

"Seven..."

The way my name fell out of her mouth captivated me. I finally spoke, for the first time since our encounter started.

"Yes, Star?"

Our eyes met again, and I could see something in her eyes that I'd never seen from another soul. Want? Love? Whatever it was, I craved it. I would have done anything for it.

"I want to taste you." Her words were smooth like honey, and all I could do was nod in approval. She could taste my breasts all day long. After Johnny had sucked on them a couple months ago, I'd been craving the same feeling it gave me between my legs.

Hormones raged between us. Star slid down my body, gently tugging on either side of my sweatpants, until my bald pussy was in view. She let out a gasp when she saw I'd taken a razor to the bush. One thing I don't like is hair.

"You ready?" she questioned, and any hope of her sucking on my tits flew out the window. She was going where no one had ever gone before.

"Miss James? Seven? Hello? We're here," Clyde calls from the front of the town car as we pulled up to the curb of Sinners and

Swingers. The club has a line down the sidewalk already. I wonder if Levi is somewhere in the mob.

I look at the clock on the dashboard - ten minutes after ten. Fashionably late, good. Keep him waiting, squirming a little in anticipation of what I have planned for the evening.

"Thank you, Clyde. Be back at midnight. I should be done by then." I tie my coat closed and open the door, stepping one high-heeled boot onto the sidewalk at a time. With a nod to the bouncer, I walk right into the club, past the sprawling line of pissed-off scenesters waiting to get in.

I make my way directly for the bar, as always. Even though I had a couple drinks before leaving my penthouse, I need a stiff shot for the last bit of liquid courage I need to pull this shit off. Not that fucking two men at once is something I haven't done before, but typically I prefer a little side of pussy with my threesomes.

Throwing back a shot of Jameson's, I turn my gaze across the room. My eyes zero in on my usual table, where I find Levi sitting casually, clearly waiting for me. The red button down shirt tucked in to a pair of black slacks fits him perfectly. Tonight, he blends in more than the first time he dared to enter the club.

The casual view of him whips an unfamiliar feeling through my body. Not only does my body crave him, but on another level, my mind does too. Subconsciously, shit is getting real in my head, without me even noticing. He catches my gaze and I slowly untie the belt of my jacket, letting it fall open. Fire flashes through his eyes as he runs his tongue over his bottom lip, like a man desperate for his next meal. The corner of my mouth turns up with the hint of a smile; my plan is already well on its way to working perfectly.

Mere steps away from Levi, Vince's dangerous green eyes catch my attention. Tall, bald as the day he was born, and muscles that ripple as far as the eye can see. His tight leather pants show his impressive bulge; even flaccid, his cock is noticeable. The black leather vest hangs open, leaving little to the imagination. A voluptuous redhead kneels in front of him, wearing next to nothing, her face almost resting on the black combat boots he always wears. Vince is an owner, and Master here at Sinners and Swingers.

His eyes lock on mine. He speaks quietly to the redhead, and she stands slowly with a look of disappointment on her face, before walking to the bar. He wastes no time making his way toward me. After my phone call earlier in the day, this is hardly unexpected.

"Mistress Marilyn. Always a pleasure, my love." He places a kiss on my cheek before playfully smacking my ass.

"The feeling is mutual, Vince. I always enjoy myself when you grace us with your presence." Over the years, his time at the club has become less and less. But tonight, he knew there was a damn good reason for him to show.

"You know, Mistress Marilyn. I have been waiting for an opportunity like this for years. You have always done your best to slip through my fingers. I haven't been excited like this in some time." Reaching down, his strong fingers grip his growing erection through the leather pants. His words excite me more than they probably should. Vince has been trying to fuck me for years. Ever since I walked through the front door of Sinners and Swingers, scorned and looking to unleash my reckless behavior.

"Give me a few, Vince. I have to speak with my sub and tell him the plan for the night." Little does Levi know that I have a big plan, which involves us both being dominated by the only man I will probably ever submit to. With a wink, I turn and head for Levi.

"Levi," I greet him, hanging my jacket over the back of the chair. He stands, wrapping an arm around my waist before returning the greeting.

"Mistress Marilyn." Impressive, he remembers the rules.

"That gentleman over there is Master Vince. He is the owner of this club, and he will be our dom for the evening." I speak short, and to the point. He can take or leave the offer; it won't make much of a difference to me in the long run.

"*Our* dom?" he questions me, his expression dark, unreadable for once. His eyes normally always give him away, just not at the moment I need to be able to read him the most.

"Yes, *our* dom. We will both give ourselves over to him for the evening. I mean, *if* you are up for it." I wink at him as I pucker my bright red lips together. His eyes skim my body from top to bottom before he turns his head toward Vince. Even though I see nothing but the back of his head, I know exactly what he is doing. He is sizing up Vince.

I lean in to Levi, running my tongue along his ear before I whisper words of encouragement. "What's the big deal? It's not like you don't like it up the ass already, Levi."

Please say no, please say no, please say no, I chant to myself, praying this will push Levi so far away that he will never try to get in my bed again. I guess I was just lying to myself, pretending I didn't care. Just leave the one night we had together at that. He turns, facing me with a lustful look. He leans in and takes my lips ever so gently. The chaste kiss is more than I expected, and I'm thrown completely off guard.

"As long as it's with you, I would do anything, baby." My gut clenches at his words. I am so beyond fucked.

My plan just backfired in my face. Now I have no choice but to go through with it all. I start walking toward Vince, as he turns to meet my strides. "Master Vince, this is Levi. Levi, this is the world famous Master Vince. He will be our dom for the night." They both extend hands while exchanging greetings.

"Why don't we continue this in the blue room," Vince suggests before turning to walk down the long hallway lined with various private suites in the back of the club. As we reach the end of the hallway, he pulls out a key and unlocks the last room on the right. "Ladies first." He smiles as I stride through the threshold, Levi not far behind me.

The blue room is one of the most lavish rooms available at

Sinners and Swingers. A large, sleek, round, modern bed sits in the middle, made with insanely soft, navy blue sheets. The walls are painted a deep ocean blue, and various toys line the walls. Whips, floggers, paddles, and my personal favorite, nylon rope. A sex swing hangs in the corner with a mirror parallel. Looking up, a mirror lines the ceiling above the spacious round bed. It is the most equipped room for a group encounter.

Over the years, I've heard tales of sprawling orgies taking place in the blue room, never thinking I would see the inside. Not that I'm reserved sexually, but I always held a four person maximum. After that, body parts get confusing and you just have no idea what belongs to whom. Not my thing at all.

Vince turns to Levi and me while he takes his vest off, laying it on a wooden bench next to the door. "The safe word tonight is lemon. If anything here becomes too much for either of you, all you have to do is say lemon. But, at Mistress Marilyn's request, I will go easy."

"Oh, I can take anything the two of you will send my way." Levi's words sound velvety smooth yet filled with bravado as he responds to Vince. The Master's eyebrows lift in question, looking directly at me. I shrug in response.

Needing further clarification, Vince speaks again, his voice low and seductive. "Will there be any man-on-man action tonight?"

I'm just as interested in the answer. I stare at Levi, waiting for him to reply; he is confused, torn, as am I. A hint of jealousy erupts through my chest just thinking about Levi with anyone else. *What. The. Fuck?* He wants to say yes, but he doesn't want the implication of questioning his sexuality after the experience. I'm mean, but I'm not mean enough to thrust him into that, so I cut in, quickly becoming territorial.

"No, if anything, I will use my strap-on to fuck Levi. But honestly, Vince, I would just rather have two cocks inside me tonight. It's been *so* long." I sound like a whiny little girl, Veruca

Salt in *Willy Wonka's Chocolate Factory*. I hadn't planned on *wanting* the experience, but since it has presented itself, I'll jump at it. Something about two cocks at once always sets me on fire.

"Thanks for clearing that up, Mistress Marilyn. If that is all the business we have, you both will strip now." Master Vince's voice leaves no hesitation at all. A shiver slides down my spine; damn, this man is good at what he does. I wonder why I never gave in to him before. Not that being dominated was high on my list of shit to do.

My corset falls to the floor alongside the barely there skirt. Before I can remove any of my lace lingerie, Master Vince stops me, eyes blazing over my body.

"Well, well, well. Mistress Marilyn. I have heard tale of your erotic lingerie, but it could have never prepared me for this beautiful sight. Leave it all on, except for the bra. Lose that." His hand grazes my back, and I feel the clasp of my bra unsnap. I slide it down my body, letting it join the rest of my clothing on the floor. Completely distracted by Vince, I hadn't noticed Levi kneeling in front of me on the floor, completely naked. *Damn, I will never get enough of his body.*

"Kneel alongside of him, Mistress Marilyn. Show your respect."

Without argument, I kneel. Something I had only done once before. The inferior feeling it leaves me with is a turn off. I crave dominance and power; it runs through my veins like a lifeline. Can I honestly go through with this?

"Good girl, Mistress Marilyn. I know how hard that is for you. In reward, I will let you pick the first move with the sub."

He surprises me. I stand, circling Levi until his face is level with my aching pussy.

"Stand up, Levi. Sit on the bed and wait there for me."

I turn to Vince, before questioning him, "Am I to call the shots with you, too, or only Levi?"

Lust flashes in Vince's eyes as he replies, "Both of us,

Mistress Marilyn. Tonight is your night." I'd be lying if I said I wasn't taken aback. Of all the years at this club, I had never once heard tale of Vince allowing anyone other than himself control. It's an exhilarating feeling.

Relief floods through my body as desire pools at my core. If the tables had just turned in my favor, I can certainly have fun with this. My stomach clenches as it completes nervous somersaults. Completely out of character for me in every way imaginable. I can't help but ask myself if this reaction would be brewing if Levi wasn't in the room. If this was just a random fuck with two men I didn't know.

"In that case, you on the bed, too, Vince. But lose the pants first. While I like to see you in that tight leather, I have been eying that bulge all night." I run my tongue over my bottom lip, and smile in his direction, completely ignoring the naked Levi lying on the bed, waiting for my next move.

Vince's pants meet the floor, and he is perfectly naked. *God Bless America, look at that gorgeous uncut cock.* While his dick is impressive in a delicious way, it has nothing on Levi's. The more I argue internally over who has a better dick, the more I pick up on their differences. While Levi's is long and thick and cut, Vince's is long and much less impressive in the girth department. *This isn't a game, Seven. "I'll take, 'Who has the better cock for $600, Alex.'" Fuck!*

I pick up a box of condoms from the bench next to the door, along with a bottle of lube. In nothing but the barely there lacy lingerie, I make my way to the bed. I hand each waiting man a condom before beginning my instructions for the first encounter of the night.

"Roll 'em on, boys." My nipples stand at attention as I watch both men work the latex down their impressive lengths. One leg at a time, I crawl onto the sprawling round bed, making my way to Levi. "Lube is for you, Vince."

I move up the bed, straddling Levi's legs and watching his

dick jump.

"Down boy." I pinch his nipple between my nails while I lower my mouth to trace the curves of his sculpted abs. Absolutely delicious. With every swipe of my tongue, I feel his hard length pressing against my stomach as I continue working my mouth up his body. Behind me, I hear Vince opening the lube.

"Patience, Vince," I snap, not even turning back to acknowledge him. Big mistake. A loud slap rings through the heavy air in the blue room; his strong hand comes in contact with my naked ass in a fit of rage. I'd be lying if I said it didn't excite the shit out of me.

I let out a purr as I eye the delicious man over my shoulder. "Mmmmm, looks like Master knows I like it rough."

Without missing a beat, Vince lands another blow on my ass, this time striking my bare cunt with his vast hand. I yelp with pleasure. Desperate to climb toward my climax, I crawl further up Levi's hard body, and take his lips. I playfully tug on his plump bottom lip before sucking it between my teeth. A grunt drifts out of his mouth; he loves every minute. His eyes lock on mine, echoing the call for need deep within my own dark eyes.

"Put it in me, Levi." My voice rolls through the room with grace, not letting on how needy and desperate I am for his cock to fill me.

His hand fists his impressive length, rubbing it slowly across my slick entrance. Back and forth, rubbing my clit, before sliding the head of his cock in between my warm, welcoming folds. Like a cat in heat, I slam my hips down, taking all of his cock in one liquid movement. He fills me up so good, like he was custom built for my cunt. I rock back and forth as I feel him bottoming out inside me. He grunts with every thrust, echoing an appreciation for my pussy.

My tits bounce up and down as I ride Levi, like my life depends on it. I throw back my head in ecstasy as the tip of his dick meets my g-spot, over and over again. I completely forget about Vince until I feel his slick member pressing against the crack of my ass. If I thought I was having fun before, this is about to go off the charts. I reluctantly slow my pace with Levi, and raise my butt in the air, giving Vince perfect access to my puckered hole. My eyes lock with Levi as I feel the cool jelly squirt onto my backdoor. I inhale sharply, never breaking my stare as I feel Vince slowly push his length in. Inch-by-inch, my body tenses. Levi can read my expression and begins to lavish my mouth with lustful yet comforting kisses. His distraction works, and when Vince is all the way in, I break my mouth away from his, panting with need.

"This is even better than I expected, Mistress Marilyn." Vince's words send a chill down my spine as he begins to pump in and out of my ass. Levi soon begins to match each thrust. And there you have it folks - a fucking Seven sandwich. As the men each have their way with my body, I feel like I am being sent straight up to Heaven. Each thrust into my body rings through my soul. My womb clenches as I feel my orgasm starting to brew.

Hands clasp around my neck from behind. Vince is close to getting off. He chokes me while he slams into my ass with sure strokes.

"Yeah, that's right. Such a tight little ass. Fuck, you feel good." His words inch me closer to my climax, and when Levi takes my puckered nipple into his mouth, I explode. My body shakes violently as the two men struggle to keep me upright while they join me in climax.

Vince is first. His pace quickens as he slams frantically into me. His balls slap my ass as he grunts into my ear with a "oh, fuck, yeah!" His hand comes crashing down on my ass once more as he rides his orgasm.

Levi thrusts up, and I move my hips to meet each of his frantic movements. He groans quietly, and holds his breath while he lets go. His thick cock pulses inside my tight pussy and I can feel him emptying into the waiting latex shield. "Fuck," I groan as I fall helplessly against his chest. Vince slowly pulls out, disposing of his used condom, while I lay sated and helpless in the strong arms of the one man I want to drive far, far away from me.

A loud knock on the door startles all of us, pulling me from my orgasm-induced coma. “Just a minute,” Vince bellows, covering Levi and me up with the navy blue bed sheet, and sliding his tight leather pants back on.

He cracks the door and is met by a club employee, pulling him out to handle an unruly guest. Something that happens more often than any of us would like to admit. Before he leaves, his green eyes rake their gaze over mine as he speaks.

“Thank you Mistress Marilyn. I really enjoyed myself. I would *love* to do it again.” Like that, he is gone, closing and locking the door behind him. Leaving me naked and alone with Levi, as I realize his dick is still firmly planted inside me, and ready to go for round two.

“We can't do this.” I drag my tired body off of him, and he looks at me confused.

“What do you mean, Seven?” He’s concerned, maybe upset? I can't read him; fuck, I can't even read myself right now. All I know is I have to get as far away from him as I can.

“Listen, I thought tonight wouldn't happen. I thought my need for another man would send you running. I didn't know this all would take place.” I wave my arms around like a lunatic, tugging the sheet with me to find my clothes. I slide my corset back on, and look around the room for my skirt.

“Seven?” His voice is quiet, meek, broken.

“What, Levi?” I snap, turning to look at him he is still lying naked in the bed, slipping the used condom off his hard dick.

“It's just sex.” His words catch me off guard. He shrugs our evening off as ‘just sex?’ Well, it is just sex, but for the first time since I started my parade of men years ago, the words '*just sex*' actually hurt. When they aren't supposed to bother me in the least.

“Yes, Levi. That is all it is. Just sex.” I pause for a moment, re-thinking everything I’d wanted this night to be. “And this was it for us. Club or no club, we won't sleep together again. This was a momentary lapse in judgment on my part, and because of our extremely close professional connection, I just can't risk this happening again. I'm sorry." I find my skirt and pull it on, following it with the boots I wore. I try and ignore him, but I can feel his gaze on me, as he works to find his own clothes, somewhere within the walls of the sprawling blue room.

"I guess I will see you Monday morning?" he questions, as I pull my jacket up off the bench next to the door. I shouldn't turn to look at him, but I do anyway. He looks like a wounded animal, and the typical '*I don't give a fuck*' attitude that I carry is thrown out the window. I actually feel bad for him; his broken look mirrors the broken pieces of his heart, and I actually care for once.

"Yes, bright and early; we have a meeting at nine." Like that, I walk out of the blue room, and head straight for my waiting car.

CHAPTER 4

Monday

Sunday, I spent the day sulking around the penthouse. I pulled my laptop out and cleared every last fucking email I had. All six hundred and seventy-three. One-by-one, I read, deleted, or acknowledged every last electronic letter. Then I took a bath, a really long bath, full of bubbles, and some strange homeopathic herb shit my parents got me, insisting I needed it to relax more. I gorged on unhealthy street-cart food from the Halal cart at the corner, and crashed, but not before downing a bottle of white wine, alone. *That makes me an alcoholic, huh?*

My car pulls up to the curb, outside the Alexander Mobile building, and I let out a sigh before exiting the safety of my uncomplicated car and heading back into the best and worst fucking business deal I've ever made. This morning, Olivia will be joining me, finally.

I brush down my black pencil skirt, while I make sure the aqua blouse is still neatly tucked in. My black Manolo heels echo through the prodigious lobby as I wave to the security guys, and catch the available elevator before the doors close.

Over the weekend, Olivia had my interior designer in to overhaul the outdated office. Mr. Stern was officially gone, so they politely packed up all he'd left behind, which will be removed before the close of the day. The elevator doors open to my floor, and I make a beeline for my office. I have half an hour to catch up, and to ensure Olivia is comfortable, before I have to deal with my Monday morning board meeting.

As I round the corner, I spot Olivia sitting at her desk, flanked by a balding asshole, flirting with her. None other than Daniel Alexander, of course. *Just goes to show the kind of creep he apparently still is.*

"Good morning, Olivia." I whisk past, completely ignoring Daniel, and slam my office door closed.

My anger can't hold long, because the office is everything I always wanted. Mikal completely knocked this impromptu project out of the park. The slim white desk sits center on the far glass wall, looking out over the city. The colors mesh perfectly. Feminine without looking like Victoria's Secret vomited all over the modest space. The carpet is black, the accent chairs are a classy, vintage shade of turquoise, and by God, the couch looks comfortable enough to sleep on. Which I will probably be doing often enough.

A note sits on the desk, with a single pink daisy.

Seven,

I hope you enjoy the office. I had fun with this project, despite your usual, unreasonable time-frame. Always a pleasure.

Mikal

"Damn, if that man wasn't gay, I would marry him," I mumble under my breath.

My intercom buzzes and Olivia giggles on the other end, not realizing the intercom has connected yet. "Miss James?" she asks hesitantly through the line, clearly sensing I was pissed off when I bound into the office a few moments ago.

"Yes, Livie?"

"You have an urgent message. Can I bring it in?" *Urgent? Great. All I need!*

"Yes, Livie," I say and kill the intercom. I set up my laptop while I wait for her to make her way in. The door opens, and she stands on the threshold. "Come in; who is the message from?"

She starts to read the notice, making her way across the room to hand it to me. "It is a message from the London manufacturing office. There is a problem with Alexander Mobile production." The last fucking words I want to hear. Ever. She hands the note over with the full details of the problem. I eye it, while she fidgets with her chin length blonde hair, brushing it down with her hands, before doing the same to her cream-colored business suit.

"Okay, I need travel set up. Book accommodations for two. I'll get back to you in an hour as to what board member is coming with me. I want the Empire Suite at the Cafe Royal hotel in London. If it is unavailable, I'll settle for the Club Suite."

I pick up the phone, dialing the president of operations in London as Livie exits quickly to prepare my arrangements. *Damn it all to Hell. I don't want to go anywhere, especially with any of the fucking board members.*

"I can't travel, doctor's orders," one of the older gentlemen says, excusing himself from the travel obligations.

"I have a three day vacation booked," Daniel jumps in thankfully, because the idea of traveling anywhere with him, especially overseas, has my blood absolutely boiling. What a fucking sleaze-ball. Drooling all over poor Livie, and she's eating it up. *Note to self - have a talk with her about Daniel, or fire her. Either way, both may be a little fun.*

"I'll do it."

The voice sends a shock through my system, and I look up to meet Levi's gaze. His hair is styled perfectly, a grey custom suit adheres to all the right places on his body, and I can't help but ogle him across the table. Without showing my nerves, I try to speak above the side conversations around the table.

"No one else?" I scan everyone's faces; they all look like they just dodged a bullet.

"If that is settled, I have someplace to be." Daniel stands to walk from the table. I still have a laundry list of shit I need the board to discuss, but no one seems interested at all.

"Ah, he who cares so little about the company that bears his name."

The conference room falls silent; all the men stare at me with shock. Clearly, Daniel walks around here like he is untouchable, but that will come to an end, now.

"What did you say?" He turns around mere inches from my face, questioning me like I have to answer to him. Wrong.

"I said, Mr. Alexander, for someone who actually bears the name of this company, you surely show little interest in its well-being and business. But I don't believe I stuttered."

Still silent, the men watch as I enter into a pissing match I am sure to win.

"I have an appointment." He is short, to the point, but I can see he's pissed. His face clearly shows frown lines as his mouth sets into a straight line, his brows furrow, and as he turns to leave he lets out a fucking huff. *Did he just fucking huff at me?*

He turns to walk from the room, but I have the last word.

"Hey Daniel, next time you miss a board meeting for an 'appointment,' you can pack up your office, and get the fuck out."

A couple men smile, Levi included. Others are sizing me up. I'm pissed. Like most men in the corporate world, they think they can walk all over me, and that just won't be happening.

"Let me get one thing straight before we continue with the mountain of business before us. I will not be disrespected, talked down to, or trampled in *my* boardroom." My voice elevates as I continue my tirade. "I am not your wife, or your side piece of ass. I am your boss. If you do not like what I have to say, or the way I do business, please, get up and get the fuck out now. It will save me the trouble of firing your ass down the line." I slam my fist on the table, "If you haven't heard about the way I do business yet, I suggest you all start asking around."

No one says a word. They stare. Levi sits in his chair with a smug grin on his face, soaking it all in.

"Now, shall we continue?"

Behind the safe walls of my office, I curse this entire trip to London. Of fucking course Levi would have so eagerly volunteered himself for the trip. Of. Fucking. Course.

My phone vibrates across my desk as I continue running over files I just received from London. I can't believe what a mess their branch of the company has become. Had I known this before the buyout, I would have never fucking bought this headache. Revenge or not, it's not fucking worth it.

Looking down at the display on my phone, I see an unfamiliar number, so I ignore it.

"Olivia," I buzz through the intercom. Her reply is quick.

"I need lunch, now. Um, get me chicken tacos from Chipotle. Sour Cream, cheese... the usual. With a Dr. Pepper." I cut the line before she has an opportunity to reply. I know I shouldn't take my frustrations out on her, but after watching her all gooey in Daniel's radar this morning, something bitter has snapped in me. Shit, that was even before the nightmare business trip I am being forced into.

A soft rap on the door pulls me from my thoughts. I invite in whomever is on the other side, since Olivia is off getting my lunch. The heavy door slowly creeps open and there stands Levi. He closes the door, then makes himself at home in the chair on the other side of my desk. He looks at me with regret and apology in his eyes. I still feel bad about the way I treated him the other night. It has eaten at me for days.

"Listen, Seven. I'm sorry. I know I shouldn't be the one going on this trip, but before you came to Alexander Mobile, I was the one doing all the traveling." He watches my reaction, as he runs his fingers through his messy hair - something I've noticed he does when he's nervous. "All the other board members have wives, and families. Then there's me. I don't have anything or anybody. By default, the trips always fall into my lap." *He doesn't have anything or anybody?* Sadness creeps through me, and I take pity on him. I take pity on no one, and yet here I am, slowly opening for a man I want to do nothing but run from.

"It's okay, Levi. It is just a business trip. I expect we'll be about a week. Give or take, depending on how quickly this can get straightened out. I have already started working on what I can from here. Olivia, my assistant, will get you all the travel details. It will give us an opportunity to see how well we work together, since it appears we are going to be spending a lot of time together." I smile at him. A genuine smile, something I rarely give colleagues, or men. A warm sensation burns through my chest and stomach as I continue to work on the file I have open on my laptop.

"Seven, I just… I didn't want you to think I set this up

somehow." He's worried, understandably so.

"Levi, I don't think that at all. You clearly didn't sabotage the supply in London. We work together; this is going to happen. We can't let what happened make things weird." I shake my head. I just don't even know where to go in this situation anymore. This is the first time in my life that I have truly been at a total loss. I look up to catch his eyes grazing over my body. He is hungry, and it isn't for lunch.

"Levi?" I ask him, looking up with heavily lidded eyes, trying to put out the fire rushing through my body, fueled by only him. I know if he doesn't leave soon, I am not going to be able to resist him. I will beg him to take me, right here on my desk.

"Yes?" He smiles at me, a beautiful toothy grin, and I can feel my panties becoming damp.

"I think you should go. I have a business call here at a quarter to seven, if you are going to still be in the office."

I can see the disappointment in his gaze, but all I'm trying to do is save us both a lot of fucking trouble. We just can't keep going on this way, because we'll only end up hurt. I can already tell he is in over his head, and despite my cool facade, he's wearing me down. Little-by-little, my walls that I have worked so hard building over the past five years are crumbling for Levi.

He leaves, and I pick up my cellphone, finally remembering the waiting text. The number is still unfamiliar to me, but I can tell it is a local New York City cell number.

When you trampled Daniel, I had the biggest fucking hard on for you. I love it when you take charge, Seven.

I can't help but chuckle as my body responds to the words, clearly from Levi, who just left. It is probably a good thing I didn't read that *before* he waltzed into my office, all sex on a stick and shit. Should I reply? Should I play into this little game we have going on here? A very fucking dangerous game for both of us.

I just can't help it, because whether or not I want to admit it, I think I just met my fucking match.

My office @ 6:45. Don't miss it. I have an idea.

By the time everyone leaves the office for the day, I have interviews lined up to replace the president of operations in London. This kind of gross incompetence won't be tolerated, period. He'll get his walking papers as soon as I set foot on English soil.

I have fifteen minutes before my conference call, and still no sign of Levi, which is probably better off anyway.

I shot Star a text, letting her know about the plans for the next couple days, and giving her free reign of my penthouse.

London for the next week. Penthouse is yours. Drinks tomorrow night before I leave?

Ideally, I like to check in with her before I leave, and in the wake of the Evan breakup, it's even more important for me to make sure she's handling it. In a lot of ways, Star is just like me. We both hide our emotions extremely well. As shattered as I was when Daniel left me, I never let anyone see. Not even Star, even though she could see right through the tough as nails persona I put on.

On cue, my phone comes to life with the conference call I'd patiently been waiting for. Still no sign of Levi; I'm sure he will steer clear of me as much as he can, at least until we hop on a plane to London and are forced to work one-on-one for days. Something I am both dreading, and looking forward to, because you know, I am mentally fucked up.

The Tokyo conference call drags on, and on, and on some fucking more. I continue looking at the clock, watching the minutes tick by, completely bored out of my mind. My participation is limited, and my need to play Candy Crush on my cellphone grows. Somewhere around level one hundred and twenty three, my office door cracks open, and Levi saunters in. His appearance is tired, his jawline covered in a blanket of stubble, his tie pulled free, and the three top buttons of his expensive dress shirt left open. If I wasn't shocked by him actually joining me, I may have found myself drooling all over my desk.

I quickly mute my end of the line.

"I didn't think you were going to join me," I state, flatly.

He runs his fingers through his dark hair, never making eye contact. "I got stuck on a call. I should have been here an hour and a half ago. Damn lawyers." Something is clearly bothering him, but I am not about to start playing Dr. Phil; I am already in too deep as it is.

My heart races as he sits down across from me, and props his black dress shoes up on my brand new desk. I should want to kill him for putting his dirty feet on my desk, but he looks too damn sexy for me to be mad.

My blood would boil if anyone else did this. I would hit the ceiling. And here he is, like he owns the place, and I am completely unfazed by it. Yup, I have lost my mind.

"Nothing from our legal department, right? I didn't get any memos." The business side of me kicks in, and I start prying, while trying to listen in on my call.

He shakes his head, pressing his full lips together in a line. "My ex-wife is trying to get more money out of me. Nothing new. Just fucking annoying." He's uncomfortable and I can see why. Who would want to talk about his ex-wife with a woman he's been hooking up with? *Wait, are we hooking up? No. It was a one-time thing. Wait. Two times. That is it!*

"That sucks. I'm glad I don't have any messy exes like that." I shrug it off, because any kind of conversation that may emotionally connect us is out of the picture. I don't need any more of a connection than what we have already established. Even that is way too much for me. The line I have always drawn in the sand has been crossed. Crushed. Erased. Pulverized. *FUCK!*

His curiosity is peaked. *Damn it. I wish I could just keep my mouth shut sometimes.* Thinking before I speak can sometimes be a weakness of mine. Clearly.

"No exes? No messy break ups? No relationships?" His warm eyes connect with mine, and I feel insanely uncomfortable all of a sudden. I don't want to lie, but the truth is more than I can bear to deliver.

"I had one, a long time ago." I shrug, and my attention is back to the conference call. I answer a couple questions before the line is disconnected and I am finally free to go home. Or am I?

I think the conversation has been dropped.

"Is it true?" Levi asks me, standing from the desk, like he is going to head for the door.

The vagueness confuses me. "Is what true?" I walk around the desk, picking up my laptop bag, and starting to get ready to leave the office after one of the longest days, ever.

"Daniel - you and Alexander? You dated in college?" His words slice through me; I whip my head up and shoot daggers from my eyes. I can feel my face turning red, something I didn't do as often as I probably should, but I can't help it, as anger takes over my entire being.

"Who told you that?" I yell at him across my office, and he knows a line has been crossed.

He thinks, very carefully before he speaks. A moment passes and he reaches for the door.

"Daniel told the board. He bragged that he left you for his wife. I'm sorry, Seven. I just thought you should know."

He doesn't move. He's waiting for my reaction. His gaze never leaves mine, and I am sure he can read the grim expression on my face. Something about Levi just breaks me; I can't hide the slightest thing from him. He is my kryptonite, and it sucks balls.

"It was a long time ago. I was over it the minute he walked

out of my apartment. He was a shitty lay anyway." I shrug it off, but I am sure Levi can tell I'm somewhat hurt. "But his actions are insubordinate, and will be immediately addressed tomorrow."

Levi smiles, a genuine, panty dropping, heartwarming smile. *Is he happy I am going to take on Daniel?*

"Good, I hope he gets exactly what he deserves. And by the way, he was a fool to walk away from you."

And like that, his back is to me, and he is walking out of my door. Ninja-mind-fucking me again, something he is becoming particularly good at.

I pick up my phone and dial Daniel's number. It rings a handful of times before he answers.

"Daniel Alexander."

"Daniel, Seven. I need to see you in my office at nine tomorrow morning, and not a minute after." I stab the end button with my finger before tossing the phone into my laptop bag. Hanging up on him didn't make me feel any better; I doubt anything would at this point. Well, maybe a fucking lobotomy? I relax slightly, thinking about the fact that I am on the verge of ruining his career, and I can feel my blood pressure starting to return to an acceptable level.

All in good time, grasshopper.

CHAPTER 5

Wednesday Morning

I step onto the company's private jet in black sweatpants, a pink Marilyn Monroe t-shirt, and a grey hooded zip-up sweatshirt, nothing but flip flops on my feet. My hair is pulled back into a messy bun, and I'm in travel mode. Unless I'm going on a two-hour trip, and have someone to impress, I travel like a bum. I want to be comfortable, especially when I'm going to be on a plane for six hours.

I set my laptop case down on the seat next to mine, toward the back of the plane, and sit down. I immediately recline the seat and get ready for my motion sickness meds to kick in. All these years and I still get sick. You would think someone who grew up living in a moving house wouldn't be so screwed up by traveling.

I close my eyes, only to be interrupted by the sound of Levi talking with the flight attendant. His voice sends a shockwave through me. I return my seat to the upright position, and notice his eyes on me.

"You feeling okay?" he asks, moving my carry-on to the

floor and sitting down next to me. He looks incredibly dapper in his custom suit, a striking difference to my extreme casual wear.

"I'm fine. I don't travel well. Motion sickness." I recline my seat back again.

"I don't think I have ever seen you dressed down, Seven." He lets out a laugh, and I decide as much as I want nothing to do with him, I love his laugh. It reminds me of a carefree child. Or maybe a teenage boy. Certainly not the businessman sitting next to me.

"When I travel, I like comfort. I couldn't imagine being stuck on a plane for six hours in some of the clothes *you* have seen me in." I poke fun at him, and myself, lightening the mood before we embark across the Atlantic.

He leans in close before he whispers in my ear, "That lingerie from the other night would have been perfect for this flight." His words send a shiver down my spine, as goosebumps spread across my entire body. I laugh and shoo him off with my hand.

I summon the flight attendant with a request before I settle in for a short nap.

"Once we get in the air, can I have a glass of ginger ale?" Anything to settle my stomach. The bubbly blonde enthusiastically agrees, and we brace for takeoff. My least favorite part of traveling.

My fist clutches the armrest, as my heart pounds against my chest. Anxiety, holy anxiety. I should have grabbed a Xanax for this. Shit. I feel a hand rest on my whitened knuckles, but I don't look up. My fist unclenches, and my fingers lace between the strong hand offering comfort. I hold on for dear life, and a short while later, we are safely in the air. But the strong hold I have on Levi's hand never breaks, and I fall fast asleep as the Dramamine kicks in.

"What time is it?" I lift my arm to rub my eyes, only to discover my right hand is still firmly connected to Levi's. I couldn't have been asleep that long.

"Noon." Four hours. Four long hours and he didn't move so I could sleep; he never gave up the grip of my hand.

I quickly withdraw my hand, and unbuckle the seatbelt, which is cutting off circulation to my damn hip. "Excuse me, do you think I can get a glass of ice when you have a moment?" I ask the blonde, before heading to the bathroom.

Behind the closed door, I stare at my hand. *What the fuck is wrong with me?* I look at my reflection in the mirror and think back to everything I have hated about myself over the years.

"Seven, you are too uptight," Blue said, passing me a joint. "You're the oddball of the family; let your hair down." My brother always could find a way to make me feel alienated.

"Leave her alone, Blue." Star sat down on the makeshift bed next to me, taking the joint from my hand and pressing it between her pink lips. "Making fun of her isn't going to change who she is. She shouldn't have to change anyway. She is fine the way she is," she continued, looking at my brother with disgust. She hated him, absolutely loathed everything about him.

"Whatever. She is fucking useless, anyway," he said while he stood to walk away, with the joint secured between his fingers. "I'm outta here; see you bitches later."

I shook my head, and thanked my lucky stars he was finally leaving.

"He is such a dick." I turned to Star and laid my head in her lap. I never got used to the verbal abuse from my older brother.

He made it clear my entire life that I was never wanted. Not by him, and certainly not by my parents. He was thirteen when I was born, and resented me every day since.

"Don't listen to him, Seven. He is only trying to get you upset." Star ran her fingers through my hair. "I'm gonna head out for a little bit. You gonna be okay alone?" she asked with genuine concern.

"Yeah, I actually think I'm going to go out for a walk by the lake. It's a clear night; I want to see the stars."

I stood up and made my way out of the old bus. I never thought I would come back hours later to my best friend, and the woman I loved, fucking my brother.

Looking up at the bathroom mirror, I want to punch it. Smash it into a thousand pieces while we fly somewhere over the massive Atlantic Ocean. I rip my hooded sweatshirt off, tossing it onto the floor of the tiny airplane bathroom floor. Gazing down at my tattoo-covered arms, I run my finger across a long, thin scar, jagged across my wrist, now covered by a vibrant blue rose. When I had all the scars from my years of cutting covered up, I privately hoped it would help to cover the memories that drove me into self-harm. The years have helped repress the memories, but they will never fully be gone.

Turning on the sink, I splash some water on my face; I pull the bun out of my hair and let it flow wildly down my back. I open the door, and return to my seat, a different person than I was when I left Levi's side. As much as I don't want to admit it, there has to be some kind of multiple personality disorder creeping within my broken soul.

"Everything okay, Seven?" He runs his gaze over my bare arms, and back to my face.

"Fine," I shortly reply.

Levi shifts uncomfortably in his seat, trying to put space between us. I guess my mood radiates through the air. "Marilyn as in Monroe, huh?"

His question catches me off guard. I didn't expect him to put it together, but I also forgot about the Marilyn Monroe shirt I'd chosen for my trip. "Yeah." I turn to face him, breaking a small hint of a smile for him.

"Mind me asking about what happened with Daniel?"

"I called him into my office yesterday." I had, and I wasn't nice at all.

"What in the fuck do you think you're doing, announcing our past to the board?" I screamed the moment he walked through my office door. Once the latch clicked, my temper unleashed. His face showed no sign of remorse.

Shrugging his shoulders he replied, "I didn't think it would get back to you."

What the fuck kind of explanation was that?

"And that makes it okay?" I stomped toward him, rounding my desk, wanting to lay him out with a single punch.

"Seven, you know how guys are." He lifted his hand up in defense.

"How 'guys are?' Seriously, Daniel? This is a fucking business, not a frat house." My pulse raced, and my face stayed pressed into a firm scowl.

"I'm going to have to ask you to leave for the day while I work with human resources on how to handle this. Please do not return until I call you." I turned, striding behind my desk and sitting down. I looked up to wave him off; he was frozen in shock.

"What?" he asked, dazed and confused. Had he thought I would just let him walk all over me? Ha!

"You heard exactly what I said, Daniel. You are to leave until I call you. This is not something that will be taken lightly. Insubordination, and sexual harassment, is a serious boardroom problem, and it will not be tolerated. You are dismissed." I picked up the phone, dialing HR, as he walked for the door.

"You are going to regret this, Seven." He tried to get the last word in, just before Ellen, the director of HR picked up the

phone.

I countered, "Not nearly as much as you, Daniel."

The door closed and I set up a meeting with Ellen, bringing her up to speed with the newest issue on my plate of overflowing nonsense at Alexander Mobile.

I explain the Cliff's Notes version of the morning, filling Levi in on Ellen's suggestion of removing him from the board of directors, something that made me absolutely giddy. His fuck up wasn't part of my original takeover plan, but it worked out perfectly.

"Wow, well, I can't say that scumbag didn't deserve it," Levi says. *Aren't these guys supposed to like each other?*

"Aren't you friends with Daniel?"

He smiles like the Cheshire Cat. "Seven, I hate the guy. Have you ever heard of the term 'frienemies?'" *Maybe Levi would be a more valuable asset than I originally thought?*

"Yeah, I guess. I never thought men actually acted that way." I shrug, and pull my laptop out to tackle some work before we touch down in London in a couple hours.

"Seven, he is a piece of shit. He cheats on his wife, and he cheats in business, but everyone *has* to be nice to him because of his position. Well, *had* to, I guess." He scrolls through his cellphone, as he types on the keys of his Blackberry. He tosses the phone onto the tiny tray in front of him in a huff.

I wonder whether or not I should even ask. If it was anyone else, I am positive I wouldn't. I care; I refuse to admit it, but I do.

My heart thumps in my ears, while I stop eying my own email, and I turn to face him. "Everything okay?" Praying he shrugs me off, I start to turn away. I feel his finger run down my arm, stopping when it reaches my wrist.

"Can I talk to you as a friend, because I think that's what I need right now. Not a lover, or a boss. But a genuine friend," he pleads with me.

I can't help but be the friend he needs right now. I lock my fingers with his, and give his hand a squeeze. "Yeah, I can be that friend." The walls I have been carefully building to keep him out continue to crumble as I repair each missing brick, another falls at the other end. I'm fighting a losing battle, and there is nothing I can do about it.

It is a scary feeling. I have been so careful to remain in control of my post-Daniel life, and here Levi is, carefully breaking down every defense I have carefully orchestrated over the years.

"My ex-wife is a real bitch. She is doing everything she can to squeeze more money out of the alimony settlement; she already gets over thirty grand a month. I don't know what game she's playing, but she's threatening me with personal shit now. I don't know what else to do." His fingers run through his messy brown hair, as he leans his head back against the plush leather plane seat, and he lets out a deep sigh.

I think of something comforting to say, but I don't have a comforting bone in my fucked up body. "Hit her where it hurts." Revenge is how I roll. I just can't understand the whole process of being upset and sappy over something when you can take charge and take over.

"I don't even know where to start. The only way to hurt her is with money. I can't get out of alimony without violating the court order. Not worth going to jail over."

Do I really have to teach this boy everything? "Did you hire a PI before you divorced?" Excuse me for thinking everyone out there *doesn't* have an ulterior motive; with my track record, I don't trust anyone.

"No, I never even thought of it." For someone in such big business, he certainly is trusting.

I try to think of the best way to put it without coming across as cold-hearted as I am. "Hmmm. Well, I'll call my personal PI once we land in London. Give me her name, and some general info. I will get some dirt dug up. She thinks she has the upper hand; you have to put a stop to that." I try to tone down my brazen attitude, but fail miserably. Maybe my lack of empathy, and caring, will drive him far away. This could work to my benefit after all.

"Once we get the upper hand, we'll formulate a plan, feed some information to your divorce attorney, and you can probably get her stripped of the alimony altogether." I shrug, and run the pad of my thumb across his fingers. "It *may* be a long shot, but most of those trophy wife bitches are hiding some kind of skeleton in their closet. You just have to find out what it is."

"Thanks, Seven." It's all he says before releasing my hand, and going back to work.

"What do you call this?" Levi asks, as he looks around the spacious foyer of the Empire Suite. The spacious pale yellow room is elegantly accented with rich hardwood flooring, modern chandeliers, and chic furniture. Two hallways run across from each other, one leading to the grand master suite, the other leading to two smaller, but just as impressive, bedrooms, all with attached en suite bathrooms.

I turn to the bellboy tucking a tip into his palm and sending him on his way. The dirty looks I have been getting from this boy, barely out of puberty, pisses me off. I don't want to come across as a complete cunt to the hotel staff, so I send him on his way. Apparently tattooed trash isn't typical in their designer suites.

"I call this exactly how I travel. If I have to be out of my penthouse, this is where I need to be resting my head at night. And with the amount of bullshit I am going to have to deal with here in London, I wasn't settling for anything less." I slide my suitcase off the bellboy's cart, and tug it behind me in the direction of the master suite. "You can pick whichever room suits your needs best." As I enter the bedroom, I can see Levi removing his suitcase, and starting in the opposite direction.

The only thing I need right now is a fucking shower. I hate flying; it always makes me feel gross. I open my suitcase, digging for my girly products, all my toiletries I never leave the country without, along with my petite makeup bag. Just enough for my less than extravagant taste in makeup. Of course, I packed them all the way at the fucking bottom of the suitcase. *Isn't that how it always goes?*

By the time I discover the bag I'm looking for, it looks like a bomb went off across the bed. My clothes are thrown everywhere like a band of gypsies ransacked the place. I really wish I had my housekeeper right about now.

I'll deal with it after I wash off the funk of the flight. I slide my sweatpants off, leaving my green satin panties in place, before tugging off my Marilyn Monroe t-shirt and tossing it onto the giant king size bed. I unclasp the black lace bra, throwing it alongside the discarded t-shirt, and make my way to the sprawling bathroom. The shower has room for a half dozen people - with no privacy at all. Two sliding glass doors stand in place next to the enormous marble Jacuzzi bathtub. It rivals my own personal tub back home. This is one of the reasons I always come back to this London gem. I open a single glass door, and turn on the shower. I grab the missing bag of toiletries while the water heats up to the perfect scalding temperature. Honestly, the heat of my showers would probably cause third degree burns on most sane people, but for me, it is nothing short of refreshing. Sliding my panties down my legs, I kick them to the side, and step in to the shower. Placing my bag of soaps on the stone shelf in the corner, I adjust the water setting and let the hot water cascade over my body.

I run my fingers through my long hair, then slowly turn around while I close my eyes, letting the steaming water run over my face. It feels nothing short of fucking amazing. I totally needed this to decompress and collect my thoughts. I turn once again, letting the water spray down my back. I lift my hands to wipe my face, and when I flicker my eyes open, all I can see is Levi, standing in the shower stall across from me, wearing nothing but a mischievous smirk, slowly stroking his erection. *Creeper!*

"What the fuck do you think you're doing?" I kind of want to punch him in the balls. What the fuck makes him think it's okay just to stroll into my bedroom, and bathroom, and invade my privacy on this level?

On the other hand, watching him slowly stroke his dick gets my juices flowing. He parts his lips, like he is actually going to answer my question, but he only runs his tongue along his bottom lip before pressing them tightly together.

A long moment passes as we stare at each other. My gaze occasionally lowers to watch the show he is putting on for me. He never makes a move for me, keeping his distance.

He finally answers me. "What am I doing, Seven? I'm enjoying the show." He pauses once again, almost as if he must catch his breath, "I came to ask you about dinner for the night, when I heard the water running. The thought of you naked on the other side of that door did bad things to me. I couldn't help myself. I just *had* to see your flesh again."

I listen to him and wonder why, for the first time in my life, someone is having this profound of an impact on me. Levi is like a drug I just can't get enough of. I want to overdose on him until I fall into a sex-induced coma, only coming back to life once he is fully out of my system, and I am once again safe. I know I shouldn't make a move, but his show has me beyond horny. I am at *needs to fuck* def-con level three-thousand.

My nipples stand at attention, as my bare pussy starts to swell with anticipation of his homecoming. I step toward him with one thought on my mind, tasting the glistening precum dripping from the tip of his impressive length. This is totally out of character for me, but even if I wanted to stop, I couldn't. My body is on autopilot and Levi is in charge.

I take another step, before I drop to my knees. I look up at him, making eye contact, as we exchange power without speaking a single word. I wrap my tiny hand around his cock and guide it into my mouth. Slowly teasing the tip, I lick the salty and sweet mixture of his arousal before wrapping my lips around his length and plunging it down my throat. Levi lets out a grunt of appreciation, while tangling his fingers through my wet hair. He grips it tightly, and it hurts, but the pain is nothing but pleasure. If he only knew hair pulling was the one thing that turned me into a wild woman, I am confident he would be pulling even harder.

I run my tongue down the bottom of his beautiful shaft as he pulls out, and thrusts back in, fucking my face at a growing pace. My free hand grasps his heavy balls, squeezing and massaging them roughly.

His body starts to tense, as he leans against the stone lined shower, never missing a thrust down my hungry throat. His balls tighten as his pace increases. I can feel the twitches in his dick, and I know he is about to empty down my throat. For the first time ever, I am beyond hot over the idea.

"Oh, fuck. Seven!" he yells, followed by a deep growl. His semen fills my waiting mouth and pulses straight down my throat. He pulls out mid-orgasm and continues his release all over my face. Stream-by-stream, his seed covers my face. It falls onto my cheeks, and in between my lips, onto my waiting tongue, while he continues to work his dick, ensuring every last drop covers my face. With the last burst of come, he turns and walks out of the shower, leaving me alone, and covered in his semen. *Well-played, you son of a bitch.* Not only am I hot as fuck, and in need of my own relief, but he just completely mind-fucked me. *Game. On.*

HERS

He sits across from me with a smug grin on his face, eating bite after bite of his salmon. I push the chicken parm around on my plate with absolutely no appetite. Still within the confines of our luxurious suite, we've opted for a room service-catered evening. After the brain beating I took in the shower, I had no desire to leave my bathroom, let alone face the world.

"You really aren't going to talk to me?" he questions, reaching for a glass of red wine sitting in front of him on the table. As the glass meets his lips, I finally decide to give in.

"What is there to talk about, Levi?"

The fact is, we have the most fucked up relationship on planet Earth. I don't want to want him, but I do. He wants more than I will ever be able to give him, or at least I think he does. And we're forced to work together in the most uncomfortable situation ever.

During the day, we opened the door for some kind of friendship, as I offered to help him fend off the claws of his ex-wife. I, Seven Fucking James, was helping a guy, whom I'm fucking, fend off his ex-wife. Ex. Wife. I might as well start waving a little white flag in surrender, because no matter the outcome, it was going to be downright fucking bad.

"What happened earlier?" His voice drips with sarcasm, as I try not to lunge across the table and strangle him to death. I'm pretty damn close.

"Oh, you mean when you came into my shower and busted a load on my face without letting me return the favor?" I try to brush it off like his actions don't bother me in the least, but it's clear that he can see right through me.

"Seven, I don't know what kind of game we're playing. But I am kind of over the game portion of things." He's trying to take charge of the situation, and in a way, it's sort of cute.

"What game, Levi? I told you it was a one-night thing. You wouldn't leave it at that. So I tried to push you away with the threesome with another guy. The only thing that did was drive you closer. I don't know what else to do to push you away. I don't do whatever this is." I wave between us with my fork, before tossing it down onto the plate in front of me and pushing my chair out. "We have to work together for this week, Levi. Please, don't make this any more uncomfortable than it is already going to be." I stand on shaky legs, praying he can't tell my body is blatantly betraying the tough front I'm putting on. My bare feet pad down the hardwood floor toward the bedroom.

I hear his chair push out from the table, and footsteps in the distance, but I don't look back to see where they lead.

"Seven," he speaks, waiting for a response. I pause outside of my door, hand on the knob. I turn toward him, locking gazes and he speaks. "Just give it a chance. A fucking chance. That is all I am asking you for."

I turn, facing the bedroom door. "I'll think about it." I close the door behind me. Fuck.

CHAPTER 6

The Night

Fuck London. Fuck this time change. Fuck this incredibly comfortable bed. Fuck it all. No matter how hard I try, sleep won't come. I look at the clock on the nightstand; it tells me something I already know: midnight. I should have been dead asleep by nine if it wasn't for Levi's question as I fled the dinner table.

He asked for a chance, but a chance at *what*? We could never have a relationship. I tried the whole relationship thing once. The whole love bullshit. We see how that worked out. As much as everything within me screams to give in to him and just give whatever he wants a try, the rational, stubborn, bitch inside me can't let it happen. The heart Daniel abandoned and shattered will never be whole enough to open up to someone. It's just something I accepted a long time ago. Not that I ever wanted that happily ever after anyway.

I roll over again, facing away from the suite door, and hug a plush down pillow, trying once again for sleep to take me. The bed dips from behind, scaring the shit out of me. My body leaps from under the covers, scrambling to turn and identify the midnight intruder.

I should have known Levi couldn't stay away. Without a word, he climbs under the covers, intruding my bed. His strong arms wrap around my waist, pulling my naked body to his. He cradles my body close to him, snuggling his face into my neck, and inhales my scent.

I don't know if I should break the silence. I want to know why he's in my room once again, interrupting my much needed privacy. But I don't want him to leave. I lie still while he curls up to me, closer than before, almost as if he is trying to climb into my body. I turn toward him and snuggle into the nook of his arm. My body starts to relax and I can feel sleep coming for me. My mind slows from its marathon pace, and I drift asleep in Levi's arms. It's something I haven't done since my time with Daniel. I pray a nightmare doesn't taunt me tonight.

Someone was inside the multicolored bus that doubled as a home our parents traveled across the country in. I could tell by the fogged up back windows. If I was really lucky, it would be my parents, along with Star's, engaging in some kind of sick and perverted sexual escapade. Ugh.

I pried the doors open, and walked up the stairs. Someone moaned from behind the thin tie-dyed curtain. The voice was familiar. I could pick it out of a crowd anywhere. It was Star.

My body went into overdrive hearing her sexy moans and pants as she neared orgasm. "Mmmmm, oh yeah," she moaned. It wouldn't be the first time I'd walked in on her fingering herself.

I pulled the curtain back. That was when I saw the most disgustingly erotic scene of my life.

Star was perfection. Naked and glistening with a thin sheen of sweat across her body, as she was up on her hands and knees, taking it from behind. My eyes scanned up his body, and landed on his face. Blue. My fucking brother. My twenty-nine-year-old brother fucking my sixteen-year-old-best friend. The woman I fucked in my spare time. The only person in the entire world that I loved.

Blue looked over and caught me staring. He fucked her harder, proving to me that anything I ever had in my life, he would take away from me.

"You like that, Star?" he grunted as he fucked her harder. Her moans picked up, completely oblivious to my presence.

"Oh Blue, fuck me!" Star called, as she bucked her ass back to meet his thrusts.

"You have got to be fucking kidding me." I choked the words out. I was so stunned. I didn't even know what else to say.

Star turned in my direction, her short blonde hair sticking to her face with sweat, and she gasped in shock when her eyes found my dazed face. "Oh my god, Seven!" she yelled, pulling away from Blue and scrambling for her clothes.

My brother leaned back on his haunches, stroking his dick while he watched Star flee, and I continued to stand there dazed.

"God, put it away. You are fucking disgusting," I yelled at him, as I turned to walk off the bus.

My moment of excitement was completely gone. Hearing her moans had me aching for her touch, but the desire was long over. The one friend I had in the world, in the arms of my enemy, and I didn't even know where to go from there. What do you do when your life crumbles?

My body tosses and turns in the spacious bed. I'm covered in sweat, and my yells echo through the expensive suite.

"Fuck you!" I scream in the throes of a nightmare. "My brother, you fucking cunt?" I throw my arm to the side, trying to slap the target in my mind, but come in contact with a strong arm restraining me against the bed. My body slowly starts to wake up, and I realize that I was not only dreaming, but also that there is someone in my bedroom trying desperately to wake me.

"Seven. It's okay. Shhhhh." His voice calms me. He strokes

my hair and my cheek, as my breathing starts to even out. I open my eyes, worried about what I am going to find. My mind catches up with the current events in my life, bringing me back to London. The expensive suite, the business trip, the man in my bed? *What the fuck?*

"Seven? Are you okay?" Levi questions, not loosening his grip on me.

"What the fuck, Levi?" I wonder why he is in my bedroom. Why he is holding me. Why does he care so damn much?

"I came in last night when I couldn't sleep. I thought you were awake?"

I was, but I only now remember his midnight visit. I look at the clock, and realize it has only been an hour since I drifted off to sleep in his arms. "I was, I think?" I start to pull from his arms, but he won't release his grip. "I'm okay Levi. I just... I need to use the bathroom."

He reluctantly releases me, and I drag my naked body across the suite to the attached bathroom. Once again, I find myself in a staring contest with the mirror. It has been so long since I had that particular nightmare grip me. Had it been triggered by Levi sharing the bed with me?

When I look in the mirror, I see a broken sixteen-year-old-girl. The girl who had her fucked up life shattered by an even more fucked up situation. Why would Star fuck Blue? Over a decade later, I wish I had the answer to that question, because it still haunts me.

"She doesn't want you, Seven. Nobody does, and nobody ever will," Blue taunted me, as I stalked out of the bus.

"Fuck you, Blue. Fuck you."

I look up, and I can see the reflection of his eyes inside my own. One of the only features we share. They taunt me with all my memories of hate for him. Without thinking, my fist collides with the mirror as I scream, "I hate you!"

The glass crashes to the floor all around me, and I can hear

Levi on the other side of the door trying the locked doorknob repeatedly. "Seven, open the door." His voice is stern, but I ignore him as the tears start to flow down my cheek.

"Go away, Levi," I yell in my rage. "Just go the fuck away!" My legs give out, and I sit in a pile of glass shards, naked and bleeding from my hand.

"I swear to fucking God, Seven! If you don't open this fucking door, I am going to break it down!" he yells, pounding against the door, and all I can do is sit and cry like a broken child. Not the strong, independent, and demanding CEO I need to be on this trip. I hear a loud crash, then another, and Levi busts through the bathroom door. He stands with a concerned look on his face, taking in the pitiful scene before him.

"Oh God, Seven." He leans down, and scoops me into his arms like a small hurt child, pulling me close to his bare chest, and squeezing tightly. He lifts me carefully, carrying me to the bed, laying me down and examining the cut across my knuckles.

I want to look up and read his face. I want to see the pity in his eyes, but I can't bring myself to make eye contact. I don't want him to see my broken soul. I don't want him to see me like this at all, but I have lost all my fight. I want to yell and scream at him. I want him to leave and never come back. I want him out of my life for good. But I can't.

"It doesn't look that bad. Let me get a washcloth from the en suite. Are you going to be okay for a minute?" His tone drips with concern, as he takes care of me like a parent would a child. A parent who actually cares about their child, something I have never known.

"Yes." It's all I can say, and I barely choke it out. His weight lifts from the bed, and I can hear the water running before he returns. I lie on top of the covers, feeling vulnerable, something I haven't felt for years before Levi walked into my life. Sleeping naked had always been second nature, but I think tonight it was the worst idea ever. However, our connection tonight isn't sexual in any way. It is deeper, and it scares the shit out of me.

He returns with a small white washcloth soaked in warm water. His hands work gently, cleaning the blood from my damaged right hand. The cut looked far worse when the blood covered my fist. It's just a little knick. The mirror totally lost that battle. I just regret Levi being in the vicinity of my meltdown. I want him gone. I want to be alone.

"Look, Levi. I think you should go back to your room." My words don't faze him at all. He continues sitting on the edge of the bed, wearing nothing but a thin pair of black bed pants, which hang deliciously off his hips. I shouldn't be ogling his muscular V, but I can't help it. It is downright beautiful. "I am fine. I can promise you that. It was just a dream." I try to let him off the hook, but he still doesn't move. *How the fuck am I going to get rid of him?*

"I'm not going anywhere, Seven. You need to go back to bed. We have a long day tomorrow. We don't need to talk about this." Of *course* we need to talk about how fucked up I am. Maybe that will send him running for the hills.

"Levi, I am fucked up. You don't want me. I promise you that. If I gave you the chance you asked for, you'd only regret it. It isn't good for either of us." I motion between the two of us. "*This* isn't good for either of us." I pull the covers over my exposed body again.

"We don't have to talk about anything you don't want to. I'm not going anywhere, Seven. Whatever this is, I'm in it for the long haul, so you can stop pushing me away."

I hate being pushed, and I hate being defied even more. "What if I just don't want you, Levi?" I intend my words to hurt, but they don't have an impact on him in the least.

"I would call you a liar." His words hit me like a punch to the cunt. A liar? I have never been called a liar in my life. There are a lot of nasty words you can use to describe me, but a liar is not one of them. I pride myself in my integrity, if nothing else.

My words come out as a whisper. "No one has ever called

me a liar before."

His fingers run along my damp cheek, and he leans in to plant a sweet peck on my cheek. "Then don't lie to me, Seven."

He snugly tucks me in under the soft covers, before climbing back into the bed behind me. His arms wrap around my waist, spooning me from behind. His semi-hard dick presses against my ass, and he presses a single kiss against my neck before tucking his other arm under his pillow and drifting off to sleep. I quickly join him, hoping another nightmare doesn't interrupt.

RING RING, RING RING, RING RING

I reach over to the phone next to the bed, answering it in a groggy daze. "Hello?"

A perky young man with a thick British accent on the other end replies, "Good morning Miss James. This is your seven o'clock wake up call." *Seven already?* I can't remember the last time I've slept this late. My body is typically awake on cue at six without any wake up calls.

"Thank you," I reply before tossing the phone back onto the receiver.

I stretch and let out a yawn. My body is achy and tired. I feel like I haven't slept at all, but I know I've probably had the most peaceful rest I've had in a very long time, thanks to Levi.

"Good morning," he mumbles in a sleepy voice, rolling over to face me in the bed.

"Morning," I reply, as I get up from the bed and head for the closet, packed with the hanging work clothes I brought for the trip. "I gotta get ready; we have an hour before our car leaves." I pull out a red blouse and a pair of white slacks, laying them on the bed before I turn for the bathroom.

"Mind if I join you?"

I don't even know how to reply to his question, but showering together after last night just seems far more intimate than I am up for. "Not now."

I wish there was a door I could lock, but I can't help but chuckle just a bit at the absolute disaster my bathroom has become overnight. I roll my eyes while thinking, *I can't wait to see the repair bill.*

I stalk into the conference room inside the London headquarters of Alexander Mobile. "Who's in charge here?" Everyone looks around, before all eyes settle on a man sitting at the end of black conference table, against a wall of windows that look over the Thames.

He nods, standing in greeting. His arm extends as he speaks. "Charles Remy, CFO of London operations." I couldn't have cared less about his title or name.

Placing my bag down on the table, I extend my arm in greeting as well. "Seven James, your former boss. Pack up your office. You're fired, Mr. Remy. Security will show you out."

I pull out my folders while everyone in the room stares at me in shock. Levi can't help but choke back a laugh as I take over London like a bull in a china shop. "Now that that's taken care of, good morning. My name is Seven James; I am the new head of Alexander Mobile, and I am here to deal with the gross incompetence of Mr. Remy and everyone here in London. I am not happy to be here. Let it be known I am not here to make friends; I am here to clean up this business and head back to New York City as quickly as I can."

I open a file folder of papers, and thumb through a couple, pulling out everything I need and slamming them in a stack on the table.

"If you want to keep your jobs at Alexander Mobile, you will help me while I am here. This is Mr. Levi Parker; he is a board member and shareholder of this company. He will also be assisting me in the cleanup of this office."

That's when I see her, a mousy blonde in the corner. Her eyes focus on Levi, completely ignoring every word coming out of my mouth. He scans the room, and his eyes fall on her in passing. Her lips pucker, pressing the pink lipstick together in a pout, as she adjusts in her seat just enough to hike her skirt up. His eyes immediately seek others in the room. My gaze burns through the whore.

"What's your name?" I ask her across the table, as her attention shifts back to me.

"Emma Malloy," she replies.

"Go set up a conference room and makeshift office for Levi and me; we will be interviewing all day."

Shock spreads across her face as she opens her mouth to reply. "I'm not a damn office assistant. I'm the head solicitor here."

"You're fired, too. Pack your shit and get out."

I eye the rest of the shocked staff. "Anyone else want walking papers today? I seem to be on a bit of a roll."

She stands and struts out of the office without looking back. Good, because I am not in the mood for loose women and their inappropriate office antics. "One thing I want everyone to get straight, since clearly you haven't heard much about me. I don't take any shit. Not from your head solicitor, or your CFO. I don't give a rat's ass. I demand respect, and I will get it, or you will get out of my office. It may not be my name on this company, but I am in charge now. I am already pissed enough that I'm halfway around the world cleaning up your mess."

This entire trip is turning into a nightmare, and I think I just fired someone simply for flirting with Levi. That was not cool at all. I'm not sure what has gotten into me, but I am sure it is Levi Parker, and I don't like what it's done to me. Well, I'm lying. *Maybe* I like it, just a little bit.

The next person in line is tasked with setting up a space for the interview process. He doesn't do half bad either. Sure, the room is about as big as a broom closet, but we have everything we need. Levi and I settle in as the steady stream of potential new CFOs flows into the waiting room. Before the first candidate enters the room, Levi turns to me. Rubbing his finger along my fabric-covered arm, he leans in to whisper in my ear.

"You fired her because she was flirting with me." He pauses as I turn to take in every inch of his face. His lips graze my bottom lip., "I can't even tell you how hot that made me."

As the door opens, he pulls away casually; the first candidate enters our broom closet. An older gentleman with a thick British accent and clearly dyed thick black hair takes a seat.

Completely off my game, I leave the bulk of the interview to Levi while I sit back taking notes, and letting my mind fuck itself for a while. All because this goddamn man is so under my skin I can't even think straight. It wouldn't be such a problem if it wasn't having such an impact on my work. This is so fucking bad.

"I called my PI this afternoon," I mention in passing as the limo weaves through London rush hour traffic.

Levi turns to me, looking up from whatever he was reading on his phone. "Yeah?"

"He should have something back within twenty-four hours or so." I shrug and pull my own phone out to send Star a text. Since the nightmare last night, I've wanted to avoid her, but she didn't do anything wrong. It isn't her fault that a decade old memory crept back up.

Levi shifts in his seat, setting his phone down on the leather bench seat, and leaning in to my personal space. "Thank you, Seven. I owe you."

I wave him off; it's nonsense really. "I enjoy seeing a desperate trophy wife take a fall now and again." I would be lying if I said otherwise. Maybe it's the fact that someone like her took so much away from me, but looking at the situation in a different light these days, I'm glad Daniel walked out when he did. That miserable housewife, perpetually knocked up, could have been me. Fuck that shit.

"I had some plans for tonight, if you're up for it." Plans? Do I even feel like going out? I know I don't want to, but honestly, I can't stay locked up in the hotel room for the duration of this trip. It will do me good to get out and see some sights. Although it's not my first time to London, every other time has been on some else's schedule, not my own.

"As long as it includes food, and wine, I'm in. What a fucking nightmare of a day. Who would think someone could make such a mess of a company?"

He smiles and turns his attention back to his phone. I do the same.

How are things back home? Bad dream returned last night. You think a decade would be enough to keep it away. God, I hate him.

Him as in my brother. It's been twelve years since I walked in on him fucking Star. It's been twelve years since I've spoken to him, despite our parents' best attempts at singing "Kumbaya" and holding hands to kiss and make up. It’s something I am not interested in, still to this day. I also drove my parents away, which doesn't bother me in the least. If I could only get them off my purse strings, I’d really be golden.

My phone chirps in reply.

Sorry hun. We can talk about it if you want? You Okay?

I don't want to talk about it anymore. I don't even want to think about it. If it wasn't for my mind transporting me back to it, I would have forgotten a long time ago.

I'm good. No need to rehash the past. Enjoying the penthouse?

Change the subject. Quickly. The limo pulls up in front of the hotel, and Levi and I exit quickly, heading for the elevators. I toss my phone into my bag as we stand waiting. The lobby is surprisingly quiet for six in the evening. The doors open, and we step inside. Levi presses the button for the suite before swiping his keycard to access the floor. I drop my bag and lean back against the glass.

My gaze falls on him. His top button is undone and his tie is loosened, just a little. His dark hair is pushed back, and he looks as gorgeous as ever. I want to run my fingers through his hair and taste the bottom lip he is cautiously chewing on. His eyes run from the climbing floors back to my hungry eyes, and we lock our stares.

I take three steps and he’s pressed against the wall of the elevator, my mouth on his. His lips part and I plunge my tongue in, massaging his in passing as I explore the mouth I’ve desperately wanted to be in for days. The elevator slows, coming to a stop. I reluctantly pull away and cross the elevator, heading back into the safety of the corner I claimed upon entering. The doors open and an older couple joins us on our ride up.

A minute later, the elevator comes to a stop on our floor. We exit into the suite like nothing happened, heading to our respective rooms. *Yup, we are fucking bi-polar as all hell.*

My phone chirps from the bag. My PI's number appears on the screen.

Miss James, my search turned up quite a bit of information. Please call me at your earliest convenience.

Interesting.

I look out of the suite. “Levi. Come here when you get a minute.”

“What's up?” He peers in my door, wearing nothing but the black slacks he had on all day. I want to lick him. I’m not even sure where the thought came from; maybe it’s my lack of orgasms lately, but damn, he looks delicious.

“Do you have a couple minutes? I got a message from my PI and it seems as though his search turned something up. I didn't feel comfortable calling without you here.” It’s the truth; this is between Levi and his ex-wife, not me.

“Yeah, cue him up on speaker.” He runs his fingers through his hair, and he kicks off his shoes, sprawling out across my bed. *Our* bed. The bed we shared last night.

“Davis Napoli,” my PI answers the phone.

“Seven James here, Davis. I have Levi Parker on the line with me as well because this is his matter.”

Levi nods and exchanges greetings with Davis over the phone. I sit down on the edge of the bed, placing the iPhone down on the bed between us.

“Well, at your request, Miss James, I did some digging into Mrs. Parker's dealings. It seems as though there is a long-standing affair in her life, as well as some massive debt.” I quietly watch Levi, but he shows no emotion.

“Long-standing affair? As in months? Years? Is there any kind of timetable on this?” His words are to the point with no emotion. In fact, I don't think I have ever seen Levi this void before. His eyes are dark, lacking any sense of emotion, pissed, which for him is a first. At least with me.

“It appears this is something that has been standing for roughly three years. The gentleman,” the phone line fills with the sound of scattering papers, “oh, here we go. A man by the name of Daniel Alexander. Married, father, lives in Greenwich, Connecticut.”

At the mention of his name, I stand and head for the door. This is more than I should be listening to; this isn't my business. Levi’s hand reaches out and stops me; when I turn to look at him, he shakes his head.

“Thank you for this information, Davis. Can I ask you to send all of this information to my attorney?” Levi is cool and collected, as I would be in the face of a business deal. While I continue to listen in, the two men end their conversation, and Levi's face turns to relief.

“Well, I guess I don't have to worry about that anymore.” He laughs as he unbuttons his pants and walks for the door. “Thanks for the help, Seven.” He slides his pants down his legs and hangs them over his arm. His ass is perfection in the tight, grey boxer briefs, and I can't help but think *God Bless Diesel* as he walks to his suite. “Be ready by seven fifteen,” he yells as he rounds the corner, and he is gone. I won't dare follow him into his suite.

I stand alone in the foyer, waiting for Levi. I chose to wear a three-forth sleeve pale pink dress that falls right above my knees. My legs are covered in sheer black stockings, connected to a sexy matching garter belt. Pink and black polka dot heels cover my feet, and I have black wrap over my shoulders and wrapping around my arms. I grip onto the small pink clutch, only big enough to hold my cellphone and credit cards. Oh, and a tube of my bold pink lipstick, a shade I rarely wear.

Levi appears out of his suite, wearing a sleek black custom-tailored suit, with a pink tie that perfectly matches the dress I wear. *Someone is sneaky.*

"Well, aren't we just a matching pair this evening?" I laugh at the sheer stupidity of it all. This is shit couples do, something we clearly are not.

"I guess I picked the perfect tie for the evening, huh?" he teases, as he holds his hand out, waiting for me to step forward and take it. *Should I?*

Against my better judgment, I do exactly what he wants. The last brick in my wall comes crumbling down, and my defenses against him are virtually gone. I am sure it won't be long until we are talking happily ever afters and babies. *Fucking ick! Crotch nuggets!*

We make our way to the elevator, and he leans in closely and whispers into my ear. "My dear, you look wonderful tonight."

I smile, as I think of the Eric Clapton song my father occasionally played for me as a little girl. Only when no one was around to witness our rare bonding. The thought sends a ping to my heart, jump-starting emotions I haven't felt run through my body in an eternity. I try to push them into the back of my mind and focus on just enjoying the evening ahead of us.

We step into the elevator. "So where are we off to for the evening, Mr. Parker?"

A sly smile presses to his lips and a dimple appears, one I haven't noticed before. Or maybe I just never got a big enough smile out of him to bring the adorable feature to life. "I have big plans, but if I told you, I would have to kill you." I can't help but laugh at him. I certainly have met my match for sure.

"Kill me, huh? Well, that wouldn't be much fun."

We continue our trip in silence, wearing big smiles. It isn't until the limo pulls up at the classically beautiful Thames River that I'm confused. "Right this way, Seven." He takes my hand once again and we start walking for The London Eye. The massive, modern Ferris wheel puts any amusement park to shame. The luxurious, glass enclosed pods are rumored to have the best views of London.

"You have got to be kidding me; I am not getting in that!" There is no way my anxiety over heights is going to allow me to set one foot inside one of those death traps. Of course, they are safe, and hell, you can even have a party in one, but I'm not buying it. At all.

"Relax, Seven. It's okay." He takes my hand, leading me up to the entrance, and he gives the employee his name. A young man with thick accent greets him.

"Right this way. Your private flight should be ready in just a moment. The capsules keep moving, some off-loading families or couples exiting in loving embraces. It's a tourist hot spot, for sure. It's also something I never thought I would want to do. However, the more I watch the carefree expressions of those exiting the experience, even on the children, the more I find myself relaxing and the anxiety fleeing.

"Mr. Parker. Your room is ready." Levi takes my hand, and we walk toward the entrance of the impressive room. As we enter, I notice a full dinner for two set up, along with champagne, and the soulful voice of Billie Holiday singing. This couldn't be any more perfect. As much as I will never admit it to another living soul, the moment I step foot inside, I give a piece of my heart to Levi Parker.

CHAPTER 7

The Date

In all my years, I've never been on a real date. Back in college, Daniel never took the time to plan anything special. I thought shit like this only existed in Hollywood. Levi never releases his tender grip on my hand as he walks me to the center of the thick glass window. I release his hand and grasp the railing in front of me as the entire room starts to move, climbing into the night sky. Lights line the outside of the spacious, moving room, leaving a low glow shining into our private space.

"The view is beautiful. The city is gorgeous at night." I stare out as far as the eye can see. Lights shine in the night sky over London. Landmarks glisten in the distance and the rich history of the city is cataloged in my memory.

"Not nearly as beautiful as you, Seven," Levi counters. *Smooth.* I want to laugh at him, but I just smile uncomfortably. I'm not good at accepting compliments on my looks; I never have been.

"Laying it on thick, Levi." I turn for the table, taking my wrap off and laying it on one of the two antique chairs.

"Hey, I speak nothing but the truth." He comes up behind me, wrapping his arms around my midsection, and nuzzling his nose into the hair resting around my shoulders. "You smell good enough to eat." His words send a shock through me, and my pussy slowly becomes slick with my need for him. Moving out of his arms, I walk back to the glass, only to discover we're almost at the very top of the Eye. His arms wrap around me once again, and my anxiety starts to flee.

I turn in his arms, my back pressed against the glass and railing. He gently lifts me and presses my ass onto the railing as a seat. We're almost level, but he still stands taller than my petite frame. I stare into his eyes, not knowing what comes next. Anticipation builds through my veins as I watch his expression carefully. His eyes show me lust, and hunger. He wants to ravish me, as much as I want him to.

"Seven," he says as he leans in and kisses me. His lips work slowly, barely grazing. His tongue skims my plump bottom lip and sucks it between his teeth, coaxing my hungry mouth open. I allow his entry, and I meet every stroke of his tongue with one of my own.

We play this game for what seems like an eternity, but in reality, it's only a few minutes. His hands start to explore my body and my nipples stand at attention against my barely there bra. As my dress shifts, I feel his strong fingers caressing my inner thighs. Remembering we are in a very public place, in a room made of glass, I start to pull back. Sex in public has never bothered me before; if anything, it has always set me on fire with want. But the fact that we are in a foreign country on a business trip kind of ruins it for me.

"We can't do this." I break our kiss. My head falls back onto the glass wall and I let out a sigh.

"Yes, we can. I paid for this private room for hours. We will fuck up against this glass, then eat that delicious gourmet meal, Seven." His words turn me on more than they probably should. But

I can't deny it anymore. I want to fuck him, just as bad as I want all the strangers on the ground below us to watch as he takes me against this glass wall.

"Fuck me, Levi. Fuck me hard against this wall for all of fucking London to see."

He doesn't need any more encouragement. Reaching up my dress, he tears at my panties, pulling them down until they slide over my heels, still firmly in place on my feet. "Oh baby, I plan on it. I've been waiting to get back inside this tight little cunt for days. I can't get enough of your pussy, Seven." His dirty talk cheers me on as I reach for the zipper on his expensive dress slacks, pulling it down and reaching in, expecting to come in contact with the sexy boxer-briefs he always wears. But to my surprise, his velvet cock falls right into my hand. Hard and leaking the littlest bit of pre-cum, anxious to fill me.

"Fuck!" he bellows as my hand starts to work him. He pulls my fist away and runs his hands through his hair.

"What, Levi?" He's clearly distraught about something.

"I fucking forgot condoms. I was too busy planning everything else." He's pissed, and so am I. I can honestly say I have never fucked without a condom in my entire life. Then again, besides Daniel, I have never fucked the same person twice.

My body aches for him deep inside me; throwing caution to the wind even more, I speak. "I'm clean, and protected."

My words wash over him in relief. "Are you sure you're okay with it?" His question lingers in the air between us as I wait to respond to him.

"Yes," is all I can say before he attacks me once again. His mouth crashes hungrily against mine as I feel the head of his dick press against my wet opening. In one frantic thrust, he drives his thick cock deep inside me. I gasp and moan all at once.

"Oh fuck!" Another moan slips from my lips as he licks up and down my neck, stopping to bite occasionally. My hands work through his dark locks, as my legs wrap around his waist, frantically holding on for dear life as he fucks me up against the glass wall.

"Oh, Seven. Your pussy is so fucking good. I could spend all night in it." God, I wouldn't mind having him inside me all night like this.

The feeling of skin-on-skin is nothing short of amazing. I can see why so many people rave about fucking bareback. I can feel every ridge and delicious detail of his glorious cock. He shifts and I can feel the head of his erection rubbing my G spot. Once, twice, and, on the third time, the orgasm crashes over me, out of nowhere. "FUCK! Levi, oh my God! Your dick is magic. Fuck me harder! I'm coming. Oh, fuck, I am coming!" I can't help but scream. His pace increases and I can feel him twitching deep inside me, as my pussy continues to grip his cock.

"Fuck!" he cries and his come pours inside my waiting cunt. The hot jets fill my pussy, and I can feel my second orgasm of the night coming. The feeling of him emptying his seed into me sends me over the edge.

"Levi! Oh God! Again! I'm coming again! Don't stop! Don't stop fucking me!" He keeps pumping into me while I scream.

My ass is pressed against the glass and the railing, and Levi is panting against my ear. The aftershocks of our orgasms ripple through our bodies as we hold onto each other.. I can feel him slowly start to pull his semi-hard dick out of my soaked pussy, followed by his come dripping slowly down my leg. This probably ranks up there in the hottest moments of my life.

He steps away slowly, tucking himself back into the dress pants. His smile could light up the dark London night sky. I run my finger along my inner thigh, cleaning the come he left behind. His dark eyes go wide as he watches every move I make. When my come covered finger dips into my mouth, he stalks forward and his lips crash on mine, sharing the mixture of our juices between our mouths.

"This is really delicious." I take another bite of the traditional fish and chips Levi had catered for our little date. I never thought I could enjoy such a simple meal in an over the top setting.

"You said you wanted to give it a try this week, so I made a couple calls to find the best fish and chips in London." I can't help but smile at the effort he went through for my meal. I think back to the plane ride over; my stomach had been grumbling and I'd made some backhanded comment about the traditional British dish.

"Finish up. Our next pass we get off."

I can't help but laugh. I've already gotten off twice, and I look forward to it a couple more times tonight. I pop a last piece of fish into my mouth, and wash it down with a sip of the divine white wine Levi picked for the evening. If there's one thing he has going for him, it is impeccable taste in wine. *I will just jot that one down in the plus category.* I'd started making an internal list of the good and bad when it came to whatever this was we were about to embark on. Firmly planted in the good category were his dick size, how he uses it, sexual openness, his taste in wine, the fact that he didn't get all huffy when I bossed him around, and well, he isn't half bad on the eyes.

The negatives are plentiful, though: the ex-wife, the fact that we work together in such a major capacity, my own personal insecurities about keeping him sexually satisfied so he doesn't have the need to look elsewhere. However, what stands out most to me is the fact that we know so little about each other. I have no idea what Levi is looking for long term. Kids aren't a priority - that much I know - but other than that, I'm completely in the dark.

Something that is difficult for me on so many levels.

I'm trying to clear my head, shaking all the cobwebs lose, when he notices I am deep in thought.

"What are you thinking about, Seven?" Levi asks from across the table, placing his wine glass down on the table and concentrating on my face. Should I be honest? The night has been beyond nice; should I ruin it with the messy details of the chance at something more than just fucking, he has been begging me for?

There is no better time than the present, right? The longer this all drags out, the more likely someone is going to get hurt. So I go for it.

"I was thinking how little we really know about each other. I mean, we know basics, but when you asked me for that chance, I don't know *what* exactly you want a chance at."

He smiles casually, like he's been expecting my loaded question.

"Seven, I can't answer that, because I don't know. I want to be with you all the fucking time. I know that. I'm not looking to walk down the aisle again so quickly, kids aren't in my five year plan, and I am still raw from everything with my ex. But when I'm with you, I can't think of another woman. When I'm not with you, I crave everything about you. From the scent of your skin to the electricity that flows through me when I lay a single finger on you. I've tried to tell myself to fuck you out of my system, but every time I bury myself deep inside your deliciously tight pussy, I want more. It is never enough. I could fuck you all day long, and want you all night. This…" he points back and forth between our bodies across the table, "this isn't going away. It's getting stronger, and I don't know what to do. Please, just tell me you will dive in with me."

My jaw is somewhere on the fucking floor. Never once in my life have I had a man go that Hollywood on me. I mean, no one has ever genuinely wanted me for *me*. Ever. I'm not sure whether I should throw my arms around him and kiss the ever loving shit out of him, or run for the hills. The latter sounds pretty damn appealing right now, but I'm still stuck in this capsule in the sky, waiting for it to descend back to Earth.

"I don't even know what to say, Levi." I gulp down the last bit of wine inside my glass, and proceed to pour another glass. "What you see isn't what you get. It has been a long time since I've let anyone this close to me." Hell, even when I was with Daniel, I didn't have the desire to let him in the way I do when it comes to this man. He has me completely fucked up in the head. I love and hate every fucking minute of it.

"Seven, you don't understand me. I don't care what I get. I want *you*. I don't want some front of who you are *sometimes*. I want the real Seven James."

Cue the emotional breakdown in three, two, one... Blast off!

"You don't want me, Levi. I am fucked up. Nobody wants me." I can hear Blue's words echoing through my mind. *"She doesn't want you, Seven. Nobody does, and nobody ever will."* I stand, picking up the wine glass and make for the door as the moving glass room comes to a halt. Perfect fucking timing for me to bolt. It would be fucking ideal if I wasn't sharing a goddamn hotel room with him. Dammit!

"Seven, don't you dare fucking run from me!"

I hear his loud footsteps behind me. My heels click across the pavement; I run as quickly as I can in these fucking shoes. *One day I will finally wear flats, I swear on everything that is fucking holy.*

I wave him off as I grip my clutch under my arm, and hold the wine glass with everything I have. What I really need is a nice pint of Jameson's right about now. I need the smooth burn of the amber liquor down my throat.

My pace slows, and my feet are fucking killing me. There is no way I am ever going to be able to outrun this guy. What a mistake I made ever getting involved with him. I feel his hand grasp my upper arm, pulling my body toward his waiting arms. The glass of wine falls from my hand, shattering all over the concrete.

"Seven, for fuck's sake! Will you just stop and talk to me? We were having such a good night. What the fuck happened?"

He's hurt. I can hear it in his voice. My body trembles against his chest as he holds me tight in his strong arms. A single tear falls from my eye. Emotion overcomes my entire being, and my soul is warmed from nothing more than his touch. This man actually wants me, in all my fucked up glory. He wants *me*. He wants little, broken, unwanted Seven James. The little girl who couldn't even grab the want and love she desperately craved from her own parents all these years.

"Shhhhh, it's okay, Seven. Let's go back to the hotel."

I start to walk, but Levi scoops me up into his arms as we make our way to the limo, waiting at the curb. I rest my head on his chest and listen to his heartbeat. Something I have only ever done with Star. I close my eyes and listen to the rhythm, *boom boom, boom boom, boom boom.* My body relaxes against his. The mere sound of his heartbeat is enough to send me to sleep. The connection between our bodies is undeniable. But can we weather the storm of my demons?

CHAPTER 8

The Hotel

The limo pulls up to the hotel and Levi exits, never allowing me out of his arms. He carries me to the elevator, and only puts me down once we reach the bed in my suite. He is tender and caring, showering me with hundreds of chaste kisses, as we both strip for bed. The night is still young. I look at the clock, which reads nine-thirty. The time change is still fucking with my body.

He slowly tugs the zipper of my dress down my back, exposing my sheer bra and the garter belt. My panties are missing, probably still inside our little glass room that I sprinted from. All I want to do it get out of this ensemble, throw on a big t-shirt, and snuggle up in bed. But I know this evening is going to send us on a different course.

I feel Levi's lips press against my shoulder blade and my entire body leans backwards, melting into his touch. I like where this is going, but there is so much more I need to get off my chest before I allow this to go any further. I shift away, standing for a moment. Confusion finds his face, as he raises his eyebrow.

"I want this. I want *us*, Levi. But..."

Before I can continue, he cuts me off. "I want this, too. No buts. No matter what you have to say, it isn't going to change a single thing, Seven."

I raise my hand and take another step back from him. "That's fine, Levi. But I need to get this out. I need you to know who I am."

I slip my heels off and unclasp my bra. It falls to the floor. Next, I remove the garter belt and sheer black stockings. One-by-one, they fall to the floor next to my bra. I stand before him, naked.

"Okay. This is me." I turn around so he can have a full view of my body. I hear a slow groan escape his lips, and my lips curl up in the hint of a smile. I turn around to face him once again. "My name is Seven James, and I am the unwanted child of two hippy nomads. The little sister of an asshole brother who reminded me every day of my life that nobody has ever, or will ever, want me." I tuck a loose hair behind my ear, nervously, and then I continue.

"No one has ever wanted me. I have never wanted anyone. I use sex to cope with the emptiness in my life. I'm a whore. I fuck most anything that walks, including my best friend. If you want me, I can't give her up." *Could I give up Star if I truly wanted to? Not completely, but the sex? God, I don't want to.* "I walked in on the only person I have ever loved fucking the only person I have ever hated. I am broken. I am emotionally void. Well, I was - until I met you. Levi, you sparked something inside me I never knew could exist. I want you. I want you to want the real me."

He watches me, never taking his eyes off mine as my hurt pours out into the posh hotel suite. He listens to every word carefully, taking it all in, and cataloging every single word I say. He is fascinated with my confessions.

"That is me. That is who Seven James is. Is that who you want?"

I continue standing in front of him, naked, waiting for his answer. He wears a poker face, and I can't read any of his expressions. My heart pounds against my chest as I continue waiting. He doesn't want me, just like no one in my life has ever wanted me.

I start to back away and he stands from the bed. He unbuttons his shirt as he walks across the room. *Step, Step, Step, Step.* His pace echoes through the suite. He stops in front of me and places his hand on my naked hip. As he leans in, closer, and closer, I can smell his manly cologne, mixed with the wine we shared over dinner.

"Seven James. I want you. I want all of you. I want you every way you will give yourself to me. I want *you.*" His words light a fire inside me, as relief washes over my wanton body. My fingers frantically move to the button on his pants, working it before taking on the zipper. He works each button on his shirt, one at a time as he steps out of his pants. Impatience grips me, and I pull the shirt open. The sound of buttons flying all over the room sends a laugh through me. He quickly silences my giggles with his mouth, firmly pressed against my lush pink lips. His mouth is urgent, licking and kissing his way until it meets my tongue. My own tongue welcomes him in greeting, and he sucks it right into his own mouth. A moan escapes through our kisses.

We move across the room to the bed, never breaking the connection between us. Our mouths make love to each other, our hands explore the exposed flesh, and our erotic sounds drift through the room as we crash onto the enormous bed. Our pace slows as we caress each other in a tenderly.

Levi's lays his body over mine. Starting at my neck, he uses his mouth to explore every inch of my body. Slowly he kisses down my collarbone, nipping and sucking along the way. His hands slide up my body, meeting my hands as his fingers entwine with mine in such an intimate connection. I feel his teeth tug on the barbells attached to each of my nipples, and it drives me wild. Desire pools within me, as my pussy becomes slicker by the moment. *I am sure he could slide right in.* I press my legs together, praying for some relief.

Finally breaking his attention away from my nipples, he releases my hands and continues moving slowly down my body. His mouth sucks on the tender flesh of my thighs before he traces his tongue up to my swollen cunt. His fingers spread my pussy open, and he dives in. His fingers probe my wetness while his mouth sucks on my tender clit. I can't keep my moans to myself; each movement has me closer to my own climax. His tongue slides inside my wet cunt and I finally let out a scream. “My clit! Fuck! Levi! Suck it!” My words are encouragement enough and he takes the swollen pearl in his mouth, sucking and nibbling on it. My body explodes under his touch and I scream my climax. I am pretty sure all of London heard every moan and scream I let out.

I open my eyes and look down. His five o'clock shadow is soaked with my pussy juices; the picture is absolutely perfect. He wipes his face on the back of his hand and starts moving back up my body.

“I need that pussy around my cock, Seven. I need to be inside you. I just can't wait anymore.” He is desperate, and I am just as desperate to get him back inside me. I will never get enough of his breathtaking cock.

I reach down between our sweating bodies and grab hold of his straining erection, as I guide him into my dripping wet core. He slowly eases into my body, pushing inch-by-inch of his thick cock into my eager pussy, taking his time. Every time we have fucked before, it has been exactly that - fucking. Quick, hard, and hallelujah, hot as fuck. But this, this is something different altogether.

He lazily thrusts in and out of me; he’s in no hurry at all. His lips press together and he slowly opens his eyes. He looks down and meets my gaze. He continues to push in and out of my center. I can feel every perfect inch of his cock, and the intimate encounter between us slowly starts to become too much for me. *Who cries during sex? Certainly not Seven Fucking James*. Yet I can feel my eyes welling with tears as Levi cherishes my body, unlike anyone before him. There is more than lust and desire between us; there are unspoken words and promises. There is *love*. No matter how much I don't want to think of the L word, and it is far too soon for either of us to even consider it, silently, it is present.

Without hurry, he rolls over, pulling me on top of him and giving me back an ounce of control between us. This simple action fills me with passion. It's my turn to show him what he means to me, with my body, because words will just never be enough.

I rock my hips back and forth, grinding down on his cock. Each movement brushes his pelvic bone against my clit and I can feel the orgasm building inside me. I take my hands and run them along my body, stopping when they reach my tits. One at a time, I tug on my nipples, rolling them through my fingertips. I moan at my own pleasure while Levi's eyes feast on the erotic scene before him. What I wouldn't give to know what's going on inside his head. Running my fingertips down my body, I only come to a stop where our bodies meet. I pick up my pace, riding his dick toward climax. My hand slides behind us and grasps his balls, massaging them as I feel them start to pull up with his own pending orgasm.

I press my other hand against his chest and bounce my ass up and down on his twitching cock. His moans increase as my orgasm starts to crash down around me. "Oh Levi! FUCK! I'm coming! I'm coming all over your fucking big dick!" My pace slows while I try to stay upright. I lose the battle and fall against his chest. I feel his dick shove into me with force, and he coats my cunt with his seed. I can feel him press deeper and deeper, bottoming out as his sperm pumps into me, burst by burst, until I feel another orgasm take me. The very feeling of his release deep inside me sends me over the edge again, for the fourth time tonight.

I am completely spent. My limbs fall around his heaving body as he pants against my neck. In between each gasp for air, he kisses the delicate flesh. I have never felt so cherished in my life, and I can't help but truly be happy. Of course, I have been happy over the years, on occasion. College graduation, my first real job, climbing the corporate ladder, but nothing on such a personal level. It will take some getting used to, but I love the feeling.

Levi's arms wrap tight around my body, and he rolls me onto my side. His semi-hard dick is still snug inside me. There's no cleaning up, and there's not an inch of space between our exhausted bodies. Just like that, we drift off to sleep.

The next week flies by in a flash. We split up the corporate responsibilities and the massive amount of problems at our London office slowly fade into a thing of the past. Today, Wednesday, is our last full day in London. We've been here a full week, and I can't tell you how ready I am to get back to my penthouse in the city. Star has been quiet, eerily quiet for her. But at the mention of Evan days ago, again, I knew it wouldn't be long until I was on radio silence again. Deep down inside me, I knew my source of dislike for Evan is solely rooted in jealousy. A jealousy that's unfounded; the reality is that Star and I will never have a happily ever after, if those even exist. What we have is purely sexual. Yeah, we grew up together, and leaned on each other. We will always have our fucked up bond of sisterhood. But the fact of the matter is that we both love men way too much.

Each night, I've slept snugly in Levi's arms, after we've made love for hours. Or just fucked. Flat out, hardcore, dirty, sexy, no holds barred sex. I have given up a tiny bit of my need for control in the bedroom, and the simple act of him bossing me around has gotten me off harder than ever before. This week, it's been earth shattering. I almost wish we could stay in the comfortable privacy of our swanky London suite. I may never admit this to anyone else, but I'm afraid of what will happen when we return to New York tomorrow, since we haven't discussed life back in the real world at all. My need for control and dominance is killing me, but I am simply trying to be laid back for once in my fucking life and roll with the punches.

Yeah, Seven Fucking James, rolling with the punches. Isn't that one fucking hysterical? I think so, too!

"Almost ready to get out of here?" Levi asks from the doorway of the closet office we've been sharing all week. "I have dinner reservations for us at seven." He smiles at me, and all the worry is gone. I hate him for being so reassuring sometimes.

"Where are we going for dinner?" I know I shouldn't question, because he has been sneaking around with this last night surprise all week, but I can't help but wonder what he has up his sleeve this time. Last time I ended up on an oversized Ferris wheel. I am sure whatever he has planned will send me into another anxiety-driven panic attack. Maybe bungee jumping? Sky diving?

"I booked one of those small private boats on the Thames. Do you have any objections to the water, Miss James?" For once, he actually spills the beans. I think I may have a damn heart attack!

"Absolutely not, Mr. Parker. I actually wanted to go for a ride on one this week, but this hell hole has had us so busy, I'd given up."

CHAPTER 9

The Real World

Our plane lands at JFK sometime around nine-thirty at night. After making it through the usual customs bullshit, Levi and I make our way to a limo waiting at the curb. Clyde is off until tomorrow officially.

I set my bags down on the curb and turn to Levi. We both have the same lingering question between us. *What now?*

"I have to go back to my penthouse. I have no idea what kind of condition Star left it in while I've been gone."

I know I should go wherever he wants, but the truth is, the last time I left Star alone in my penthouse, I came back to a fucking disaster. I'm a little worried about the condition this time around.

"That's fine. I'll come along, as long as you show me your real bedroom this time." He jokes, thinking back to our first night together. I could totally have some fun with that toy closet tonight.

I laugh and joke back, "You're pushing it now, Mr. Parker. First, my bedroom, then you are going to want to move in!" *Not that it doesn't sound like a great idea; on second thought, it scares the shit out of me. FUCK! Why am I even thinking about any of this fucking nonsense! So much for playing it cool, Seven!*

His eyebrow raises, and his face grows serious.

"Oh, that is something I plan on taking about, and soon."

I want to laugh, but I don't think he's joking. The limo driver takes our suitcases and shoves them into the trunk, and I give him my address. We simultaneously scroll through our phones, catching up on anything we missed while we decided to nap during our flight across the Atlantic. A moment later I hear Levi talking quietly; I ignore it as much as I can, being in an enclosed space together. I have an email from human resources, requesting a meeting tomorrow morning upon my return to the office. I reply and schedule for bright and early.

I hope this is regarding the resignation from Daniel, but my life never works that easily. The limo comes to a stop in front of my penthouse, and we both head for the lobby without waiting for our bags. "Jesse, can you send those up?" I ask the trusty night guard as I head into the elevator. Levi follows closely behind, still engaged in his phone conversation.

"I'm in an elevator. I'm going to lose you. We will continue this in the morning." He disconnects the line, shoving the phone into his jacket pocket.

"Everything okay?"

He shrugs. "Ex-wife. That was the lawyer."

The elevator chimes and the door opens into my foyer. I stop dead in my tracks when I hear moans echoing through my house. I look at Levi, and he looks back at me, equally stunned. I just spent fucking six hours on a plane, and this is what I come home to?

The screams get louder, and I'd know the voice anywhere. Star.

"That woman is Star; the man is to be determined." I stomp down the hallway heading directly for my playroom. "Un-fucking-believable," I mumble under my breath.

I stop at the door, looking back at Levi, before we both burst through the door at the same time. Spread across the large bed is Star, with not one, but two men fucking her. One man I recognize immediately. Stuffy Evan who pitched a fucking fit when I would fuck Star. The other man I don't recognize.

“What the fuck, Star?”

All three heads snap in our direction. That’s when I immediately know who he is. The second man. One of the two men in the entire world whom I can say I truly fucking hate. My brother, Blue. And the worst part of it all? He is still fucking her as if I’m not standing here, in my fucking penthouse, where *none* of them are welcome anymore. How could she think this would be okay?

“I'm sorry, Seven. I didn't know you were back yet.” *Because that makes it okay.*

She pushes Blue away, and he falls back onto the bed. My fucking brother. Is naked. On the bed I use to fuck. I want to vomit everywhere, but I somehow contain it within my own mouth.

“All of you… get the FUCK out of my home. You are NOT welcome here.” I look Star in the eye, and press my lips together. “And YOU! I am done with you. All these years later and you do this. Again! You are DEAD to me! Do you fucking hear me? DEAD!”

My chest heaves as I struggle to catch my breath. I stomp out of the bedroom and head for the kitchen, the freezer specifically. Levi is hot on my trail. I can hear Star sobbing from the back bedroom, and something inside me breaks. I just don't care. The one person I’ve loved unconditionally for virtually my entire life, has once again betrayed me, in the worst way. I can't bring myself to look at her, or talk it out again. It may have been a long time since the first time I caught her with Blue, but now that it is front and center, in my own fucking home, I know for a fact this isn't something that only happened once or twice.

Levi stands in the entry of the kitchen, shielding me from

the men leaving. My brother stops behind Levi, and I can see out of the corner of my eye how protective Levi has become.

“Fuck off. She is my sister and I want to talk to her,” Blue mouths off at Levi. He doesn't reply, but he doesn't back down. He simply waits for my reaction.

“Blue, you aren't anything to me. Get the fuck out of my home.”

Levi turns toward Blue, and I watch attentively. My brother clearly hasn't been taking care of himself. His light brown hair is greasy, hanging just below his eyes. He has lost a lot of weight since the last time I saw him, but then again, it was so long ago that I don't even know what normal is for him anymore. But the most notable thing about him is the fact that he is clearly strung out.

“You heard Seven. She said get out. If you don't leave willingly, I will have you hauled out of here by the fucking police.” Levi is trying to be polite, and I can tell he’s holding back. His fists clench at his sides as he sways from one foot to the other. I open the freezer and pull out the bottle of Jameson’s I have hidden behind the ice machine. I unscrew the cap and bring the entire bottle to my lips. I take a large swig and shake it off as the amber liquid burns down my throat, giving me a moment of clarity. It used to be Seven and Star against the world, and now a very bright half of the dynamic duo is gone. For good.

Star walks past the kitchen and I can hear her sniffles. “I'm so sorry, Seven. I never wanted you to find out. I am so sorry.” She continues crying, as she tries to make it into the kitchen, to me.

Levi stops her and her mood shifts. Instead of crying hysterics, she could spit venom.

“Who do you think you are?” she yells at him, as she tries to push past him to no avail. “She will walk away from you just like she walks away from everyone else in her life. She will leave you with nothing. Broken and alone. That is what Seven James does. She doesn't love. She destroys.” I must admit, her performance is Oscar-worthy.

He laughs in her face, taunting her. “Well, I guess if she walks away from me, I will be bitter and heartbroken. But one thing I won't do is betray her like you have.” Before I can see what happens, I hear a loud slap echo though the bare kitchen. She slapped him, right across the face.

“GET THE FUCK OUT OF MY HOUSE!” I scream at the top of my lungs, then crumple into a ball on the tile floor. Star walks into the elevator, and out of my life. Hopefully for good. I can't move. I just sit on the kitchen floor with my legs closely pressed to my heaving chest, my arms tightly wrapped around my knees. Dazed and confused. Wondering how my life became so fucked up.

I hear his footsteps before Levi sits down next to me on the floor. He wraps his arms around me and whispers into my ear, “I am so sorry, Seven.” I lean my head against his shoulder, and just let him hold me. His hands rub up and down my arms. I need this, more than I could ever imagine. What would I have done if I came home, alone, to that? Sometimes fate has a fucked up way of throwing people together, but I know whatever it is that Levi and I have, I need it.

In the past ten minutes, I went from having an awesome, lifetime best friend, to being alone with a man with whom I have no idea what the future holds, and it scares the shit out of me.

Ring Ring, Ring Ring, Ring Ring, Ring Ring, Ring Ring.

My phone won't stop ringing. I look over to see a picture of Star on the display for the fifteenth time tonight. She is relentless, but I refuse to pick up the phone. After every call, she sends me a text, knowing I will read it. Because I am just a fucking glutton for punishment. Always have been. It is like a train wreck; I just can't help but look.

I am so sorry. Please hear me out.

Seven, please don't throw our friendship away over this.

You don't understand. This isn't how I wanted my life to be.

Please, just talk to me.

The list goes on and on. I am exhausted, and I just want to go to bed. I turn my phone off, not caring if I miss anything important, business-related. They can get a hold of me in the morning, when I return to reality.

I curl up in the arms of Levi, and for the first time since he climbed into my bed a week ago, I don't sleep soundly. I toss and turn, keeping him up all night. Somewhere around four in the morning, my body says fuck you and throws me into a coma until my alarm scares the shit out of me at a quarter to seven. I can already tell this day is going to fucking suck.

"Miss James, come in. Have a seat."

Kate Harris is an older woman, slightly grey around the edges of her dark chestnut hair. She wears a pair of thin, metal-framed glasses she continuously pushes up her nose, and for some unknown reason, she has a pencil stuck in her hair. Not exactly a fashion statement, but whatever.

"Thank you for handling this all while I was called away in London. If you could have even seen the mess over there..." I let out a small laugh while I sit down in the office chair, cross my legs, and wait for her to begin the meeting I was dragged into this morning. My first morning back in the States, when I have a disgustingly huge pile of shit to sift through on my desk.

"We have taken your complaint very seriously, Miss James. While you were gone, Mr. Alexander was asked to take a short leave of absence as we worked internally to find the best remedy for the situation. Seeing as he is part owner of the company, we just can't fire him." She's pissed; I can tell already. Maybe Daniel came on to her over the years, too. She's older but it seems like his taste is anything with a vagina.

She takes her glasses off, and rubs her eyes, clearly stressed, before picking them up and putting them back on. "We have very little in terms of options. The other board members have not opted to buy out his shares. They are loyal. We can offer him a severance package, but cuts would have to be made all around the company, and I don't see that being a wise choice." She pauses again, and I think it finally sinks in. She's telling me there is absolutely nothing she can do about this whole fucked up situation with Daniel.

"Unfortunately, Miss James, there is nothing we can do." Of course. I should have known better than to think taking the high road would ever get me anywhere. But karma is a bitch; in fact, it is one of the only beliefs I have in my fucked up life. So I am going to continue waiting for the universe to bite Daniel Alexander right in the ass.

"I understand, Kate. You did what you could; unfortunately, it is an uncomfortable situation all around when someone like him is untouchable. I appreciate all of your hard work while I was away. If that will be all, I am going to go tackle the giant pile of work I need to get through today." I leave her with a polite smile. No need to take my rage out on her, since she did nothing wrong. If anything, she went above and beyond her own job description trying to get rid of this fucking menace.

I open the door to my office, only to find Levi sitting in my chair behind my desk. *Oh you know, just fucking make yourself at home.*

“Not in a better mood, I see.” He is observant, for sure.

“Meeting with HR didn't go as I would have liked. Looks like we are stuck with Daniel.” After the words leave my mouth, I can't help but remember the news Levi got while we were in London, about his ex-wife carrying on a long term affair with Daniel. I feel bad bringing him up, but he doesn't look affected by it in the least.

“Come here. Let me make you feel better.” His words drip with lust, and I can't help but think about last night, how it had been the first night in so many when we didn't ravish each other the moment we hit the bed. Every night in London had become an opportunity for us to explore each other’s bodies. Our boundaries. Our sexual wants and needs. All of which vanished the moment I stepped into my penthouse.

I lock the office door and walk to the desk. As I round the corner, I would like nothing more than to christen it. The vision I stumble upon is something I will never forget, as long as I live. Levi has unfastened his belt, the top button of his dress pants is open, and his big dick is free of the restraints of the zipper. His hand slowly strokes up and down his length, all while watching me with hungry eyes.

Without a single thought, I hitch my skirt up and slide my pink lace panties down to the floor, kicking them off the toe of my Jimmy Choos before climbing onto his lap and straddling his strong thighs.

“You know what I love?” he asks me, as I move closer to his mouth, leaving enough room so we don't touch.

“What?” I breathe out.

“The way that you come to me, without a single word or command. Like you are mine for the fucking taking; I always thought I would be the one belonging to you.” His words hit me like a slap to the face. He’s right. All the time I spent telling myself that I would stop at nothing to dominate him, and anyone I ever came in contact with sexually, and here I am, just as submissive as some of the men and women I've fucked over the years. The most troubling part of it all? I'm not scared.

"You bring out this side of me, Levi," I whisper into his ear as I sink my wet pussy down onto his rock hard cock. I slowly move up and down, taking in every glorious inch that fills me so perfectly. A little too perfectly.

"I love the way your tight cunt grips my dick. It's like your pussy was made for me. Only me," he chokes out as his breathing hitches and he starts bucking his hips up to meet my pace.

His words make me even hotter than the fact that we are fucking in my office, something I would have never considered doing. Work and sex have always been two different worlds.

"My pussy was made for you." My body is on autopilot; so is my mind. I don't know what I am saying, because I am lost in the delirious frenzy of the orgasm I desperately need. I grind my cunt down on him, and that is when I feel it. He grabs my hips tightly and slams my pussy down onto his cock. I feel his orgasm emptying into me, and the pulsing of his dick sends me into my own world of orgasmic bliss.

I scream. Loud. So loud that Livie knocks on my door, asking if I'm all right. I stay in the same position I've been in for several minutes, spread eagle on Levi's lap, in my office chair, with his come dripping out of my pussy. Any hint of a foul mood is now gone. All thanks to Levi. *Fuck, now to explain that to my assistant!*

I buzz Livie on the intercom and ask her to come in for a meeting once Mr. Parker leaves. Of course now I need to think of some kind of an explanation as to why I sounded like a fucking porn star behind the closed door of my office. Maybe the threat of firing her, or a raise. *Yeah, a raise, that will work!*

We share the en-suite bathroom while we clean up our mid-workday quickie.

Levi heads on his way, and I sit down for hours of work. By lunchtime, I haven't budged, and it seems like the ocean of work is only getting deeper. I should just hire someone to do this shit for me. Now *that's* a good idea. *Note to self: get Livie to hire yet another fucking assistant.*

I have lunch delivered and even though I can still feel Levi's delicious release inside my body from this morning, my mood is getting worse and worse. Around three, my office intercom buzzes, and Olivia comes to life on the other end. Happy as usual. "Miss James, Star is here for you."

The last thing I want to deal with. Why in the fuck would she come to my work? She fucking knows better than to ever bring her bullshit into my office. All these years, all these mother fucking years, and she decides she has to corner me in my office?

"Send her in."

When she walks through the door, I can tell she's been up all night; her hair is pulled up in a messy bun on the top of her head with loose strands falling all around her face. Her face is bright red, like she hasn't stopped crying. The beautiful brightness in her blue eyes is gone, replaced with a void look of desperation, and she's wearing the same clothes she left my penthouse in the night before. Then I see them. The bruises. There is a large one on her upper thigh. A handprint across her face, which was hidden by the redness of her cheeks. A small purple mark at the side of her eye and, when she removes her coat, I see them clear as day. Two large bruises around her neck. The kind of marks left behind when someone really wants to do some damage.

My heart stops. I am still so mad at her, but every protective gene in my body kicks in, and I have only one question. "Who did this to you, Star?" As much as I am still really fucking pissed about her betrayal, I can't bear to see her, let alone anyone, on the receiving end of this kind of a beating.

"Blue." She collapses into the chair in front of my desk and the crying begins. "Seven, I didn't want to. I never wanted to. But he threatened to tell everyone what I did. He has held it over my head for years." She makes absolutely no sense. What could he hold over her head that I wouldn't already know? Maybe a secret from our parents, but in all the years we have been Star and Seven, she has never kept anything from me.

Her sobs get louder, and her hands come up to cover her face. Her entire body heaves as her breathing becomes labored, and then she says it. "Seven, I had a baby. Blue's baby. The year you left for college."

Shocked isn't the right word to describe my feelings. I am appalled and sickened. I am hurt and saddened. I am furious and seething. But what I am mostly surprised at are my feelings of pity and concern for the broken woman sitting across from me. The woman who has needed me more than I have needed her throughout our lives. I feel responsible for letting that scumbag get his hands on her. I should have been able to protect her, just like I should have protected her last night instead of kicking her out.

I come around my desk, and pull her up from the chair, wrapping my arms around her body and holding her as tight as I can. Hoping I'm not hurting her. She cries and cries. One of those ugly cries. I just stand and hold her.

"I'm so sorry, Seven. I never meant to hurt you." The last thing she needs to be doing in her state is apologizing to me. That is for damn sure.

"It's okay Star. He won't hurt you again. I will make sure of that. I am going to have Clyde take you to my penthouse until I get home. You are also going to fill out a police report detailing exactly what he did to you." She nods, and gathers her things.

"And Star?" She turns back to me, a small smile trying to poke through the grim expression plastered to her face. "Where is the baby?" I know it is probably the wrong question to ask, but I can't stop thinking about the child who is out there somewhere. God, it would have to be almost ten or eleven.

She wipes a tear from the corner of her eye, "I don't know, Seven. After she was born, my parents took her to a commune upstate, and I never saw her again. Christmas Day, she will be eleven."

She turns and walks out the door, and I sink into my office chair feeling like the weight of the world has just been dropped on my shoulders. First Blue will pay, and then I will find this little girl who was taken from Star. Looking at the clock on my computer, I notice it's been over an hour. I have a meeting to head to, and sometime before the end of the day, I need to explain my new house-guest to Levi, who apparently is becoming a more permanent fixture around my penthouse.

CHAPTER 10

Sharing

My phone buzzes with a text from Levi as my town car pulls away from the Alexander Mobile building.

Meeting with PI and my lawyer, will be a little late. See you around 8.

Clyde slows the car at the curb of my building, but before I step out, the partition slowly rolls down, and the friendly older man, who has been a trusted employee for years speaks.

"Everything okay Miss James?" He is concerned, concerned like a father should be. Something I have never experienced from anyone, not even my own father.

"Yeah, Clyde. Life is good."

Until I self district, I should say. But, I don't.

When I walk into my penthouse, I see a small bag by the couch. Star's overnight bag is open and a couple pieces of clothing are pulled out. I hear water running in the distance, and hope she is using the guest bathroom because all I want to do right now is take a damn shower, throw on a baggy pair of sweatpants, and veg out until Levi comes in for the night. I feel like I have been hit by a

Mack truck of work. The worst part of it all is that I still have more to do tomorrow.

I walk into my bedroom to see clothes on my floor, and I know she's using my shower. It's big enough for a small army, but with the events of the day, would it really be a good idea to go and jump in with her? Granted we have been showering together since we were like five years old, but after the fallout of the past day, I just don't know. Then my slut charged mind kicks in. *Seven, go take your shower, in your fucking shower. She is lucky you are going to forgive her, for fuck's sake!*

I open my bathroom door, and the room is full of steam. The mirrors are all fogged up, and the glass doors of the shower stall are the same. I can hear her humming to herself, and I recognize that her mood has improved some since she left my office. I worry about her, and now her years of depression seem completely justified. I'd always thought the worst. Like someone had abused her as a child, because given the crowd our parents ran with, I'm downright surprised we hadn't been targets.

"Star?" I say, while I start to unbutton the blouse I wore for the day.

"Seven? You're home." *Was that a question?*

"Yeah, I need to get in there. It has been quite the damn day." I continue to undress, and wait to hear the water turn off and see her step out of my shower. But she doesn't. "Are you okay in there, Star?" She is unusually quiet, and I battle between opening the foggy glass doors, or just hightailing it to the other bathroom down the hall.

"I'm fine, Seven. Are you coming in or not?" Well, I guess that answers that question. I stand at the glass doors for a minute debating whether or not this is a good idea. I mean, of course, I think she is attractive, but I'm still kind of mad at her. At least I don't have a dick that would give my arousal away.

Against my better judgment, which is a pattern in my life, I open the door of the shower.

I stop in my tracks when I see her. Completely naked, white suds covering her body. One hand rests on one of her large breasts; the other falls somewhere between her legs. I don't know if I should turn and look the other way, or get out. I do neither.

I can feel moisture pooling between my legs, and I can tell you for fucking certain that it isn't from the showerhead I just turned on. Her gaze never leaves mine, and we stand and stare at each other for minutes.

"Like what you see, Seven?" she speaks and my knees could buckle. *Like what I see?* Fuck, yeah. When have I *not* liked that hot little body? I can't form words to answer her question, but I nod.

"It has been so long, Seven." She moves a step toward me. Her words remind me of just how long it's been since I've felt her body pressed against mine. Evan wouldn't share, and I hated him for that.

"It has," I reply.

She takes another step toward me. My pierced nipples stand at attention, goosebumps spread across my skin, and my breathing slowly increases. "I've missed you, Seven." Another step, and her breasts press against mine. She leans in, and I can feel her breath on my neck. "I want you." Her words are clear as day; they send a shiver through my body. She knows I want her just as much as she wants me.

"Star," I start in protest, Levi entering my mind, but before I can say anything else, her lips are on mine. She licks and sucks on my mouth, all while pressing her slick soapy body against mine. Our nipples graze each other's and I feel my clit throbbing with need for relief.

Her lips pull away, and I have to get the words out. "Star, share. You have to share. I can't be yours." But my declaration doesn't stop her. She continues her lips down my collarbone, heading right for my breasts. My hands run through her wet, silky hair as she takes one of my nipples in her mouth. Pleasure fills my body as she sucks on my tit, occasionally tugging on the barbell with her teeth. Her free hand snakes between my legs, inserting one finger at a time into my soaked cunt.

Her lips continue down my body, cherishing every inch with divine licks and kisses, only stopping when she comes to my glistening pussy. Wet and ready. My back is firmly pressed against the wall, as the warm water continues cascading around us. Her fingers part the lips, and her tongue licks and teases my tender clit. The minor contact sends my body into overdrive. My lips part and moan in appreciation. It feels so fucking good. Her mouth teases and nibbles on my bud, before her tongue slowly dips inside my center.

"Oh God! That feels so fucking good." I can't help myself. Shit, I have missed her mouth on my cunt.

"What the fuck?" I hear a deep voice bellow from outside the glass doors, just as the door swings open. Levi stands there, clearly seeing red. Until his eyes land on Star.

I jump, and Star pulls away. We both stand there, looking at Levi, waiting to see what is going to happen next. "I told you, Star. You have to share." I nod at Levi, who is standing there with his mouth hanging open.

"I'm sorry, Levi. But if you want to join us, you are welcome. We were kind of..." I pause for a second, thinking of the right way to describe what he just walked in on. "Making up."

He starts pulling at his clothes, like he can't get them off fast enough. "One rule." I speak up, as my mind starts racing with what is about to happen. I've had threesomes in my time, but none with anyone that has meant an ounce of anything to me. "You must wear a condom if you fuck her. You can bareback me all you want. Her, no dice."

He nods and continues to strip down. As his boxer-briefs fall to the floor, Star lets out a gasp. "I guess that is why you keep this one around," she giggles and continues staring at his gorgeous cock. If she only knew it was so much more than his impressive dick. "Come here, Levi." For the first time in my life, I feel something new. Jealousy. Possession. I don't want to share him with Star, or anyone. What would have been a fun game to me before is quickly becoming something that just may send me into a rage.

I push the irrational feelings to the back of my mind, and claim what's mine.

"Fuck me, now. Up against this wall. Hard and fast."

His arms wrap around my waist, and I wrap my legs around him, pressing the heels of my feet into his ass. Star stands alongside us, watching, as her fingers roll over her clit and push inside her wet pussy.

In one hard thrust, Levi plows his dick completely inside of me. I feel him bottoming out but he doesn't slow down one bit. He follows instructions carefully, fucking me hard against the shower wall. His hand reaches between us, grazing his thumb over my swollen clit, and I can feel my release come crashing down around me.

"Fuck! Levi! So fucking good. Fuck my pussy good!"

He continues thrusting inside me, harder with each push. "Your pussy is fucking heaven," he says, as I feel his dick find his release deep inside me. "Oh fuck," he whispers against my neck, before his lips collide on mine. He feasts upon my mouth while his dick coats my pussy with his seed, cuing my second orgasm of the night. I pant into his mouth, trying to catch my own breath, completely forgetting about the audience next to us until Star starts moaning in her release. She watches us fuck, as she rides her own fingers, and I think I could die from how fucking hot it is.

He slowly pulls out of me. Without a second thought, I instruct Star, "Lick my cunt clean."

Levi grunts, and his hand reaches down for his semi-erect cock and begins stroking as Star lowers to her knees in front of my soaked pussy. She wastes no time getting to work, licking and sucking on my used pussy, cleaning every ounce of Levi's come from me. My clit hums in appreciation, and my body is ready for another release.

With my cunt still in her mouth, Star speaks. “I want a ride on that.” She motions to Levi's dick, and I see red. What started as a fun idea with two people I care about is quickly becoming no fun for me at all.

“I’ve got a better idea.” Quick thinking on my part, but there is no way I am letting him fuck her, condom or no condom. He is mine, and mine only.

“This is what we are going to do when we get out of here. First, I am going to get my strap-on. Then I am going to fuck you, while Levi fucks me.”

Star nods in agreement.

The bed dips and Levi wraps me in his arms. He slowly showers kisses all over my body, cherishing every inch of my being. We lay tangled in each other’s embrace until Star returns from the spare bedroom, *her* bedroom, where she will be sleeping once this night is over. I’m still unsure why I agreed to this, because it’s still sitting wrong with me. Maybe I just wanted a little piece of Star before I set her free. It feels cruel and uncaring, but I am at a crossroads of my life I never thought I’d see. In the night silence I have had the smallest coming to Jesus meeting of my life.

The only bit of comfort I take away from any of it is the fact that Levi has shown no interest in Star. Only me. His silent support of my antics has completely mind-fucked me. Everything about my life in the past month has left me questioning everything I’ve ever wanted, or believed in. My path of life. My choices for life. Everything.

And now I lie here, between my naked best friend who has fucked me over more than I will ever know, and the naked man whom I would give up anything for. Ain't life fucking funny? It has a strange way of just creeping up on you and slapping you across the face.

"I can't do this." I sit up in the bed between Star and Levi. They both stare at me. Levi is filled with compassion, and what looks like relief. Star, on the other hand, is hurt, as I knew she would be. Rejected again in life; it's something I have felt on so many occasions. My heart breaks for her. "I'm sorry, Star. I love you, and I always will, but I just can't do this anymore. I never thought there would be a day when I just couldn't share anymore. But I've found it."

"It's okay, Seven. You don't have to apologize for finally finding happiness in your life. I can tell by the way you look at him. He's good for you." She gets up and pulls a long white robe off the chair and slips into it. "You will always be my best friend, no matter what. We may not be little kids anymore, but you will always be my sister." Her back turns, and out the door she goes. Her feet pad down the hallway until I hear the click of the door telling me she is in there.

"Are you okay, Seven?" Levi's voice reminds me that I'm not alone, even though my brain is in overdrive.

"I don't know," I whisper, and his arms wrap around me again. His touch comforts me, and so do his words.

"I'm glad you stopped that. The only person I want is you. But I would do anything for you, Seven. Anything."

I snuggle into the comfort of his arms, wondering what I have ever done in my life to deserve someone who is so good to me.

"Davis? This is Seven James." I sit in my office the next morning on the phone with my private investigator. During the night, when Star couldn't sleep, she came to me. I slid out of bed and lent her a shoulder to cry on as she spilled the story.

"Seven, after that first time, when you caught us, he wouldn't stop. He continued to force me to sleep with him me for two years. I liked it at first, but he got violent; he treated me badly. Then I got pregnant, and he wouldn't come near me again."

Her words hurt. My brother had raped her, over and over again. He'd broken her. He'd broken her spirit. He'd broken her soul. He had taken the light from her eyes. He'd taken her innocence.

"I want to find her. I want to find Willow."

That was all she needed to say. I would stop at nothing to find the little girl she's been forced to hand over.

"I have an extremely important missing person project. I need to find a child. Her birth date is December 25, 2002. Name on her birth certificate will be Willow James. But the name could have been changed. Birth mother is Star Bloom. Birth father is Blue James. Birthplace should be Woodstock, New York." It was all the information I had; it was all the information Star had. When her little girl had been three days old, our parents together had taken her and adopted her out to another hippie couple in the small community we ran with over the years. I doubt there had been anything legal, much less a paper trail. But if there was something, Davis would find her. I would put Star in contact with him, and let her go.

Her plans included leaving on Friday to head upstate to the

last place she remembered being with her daughter. It was something she needed to do to move on. Just like I had to let her go so I could move on with *my* life. It's something we both should have done a long time ago, but neither of us had been ready. The things that change over time are always so confusing in life.

A quiet knock on the door catches my attention, and I quickly end the call with Davis. Looking up, I see Daniel standing in the doorway of my office with his typical smug grin on his face. Since there was nothing more HR could do, they invited him back into the office, effective today. Apparently his first priority is fucking with me. *Game on, cowboy, because I am in a foul ass mood.*

"Can I help you with something, Mr. Alexander?" *Business. Keep it fucking business,* I tell myself. But it is so fucking hard when I want to just punch him in the face.

"Nice to see you, too, Seven. How was your trip?" He plops his ass into the chair in front of me, kicking his ugly ass shoes up on my desk. *Strike two.*

"It was informative, for sure. Got a lot done. Thankfully, we won't lose millions over their shortcomings now." I focus on business, although I'm sure he is trying to pull some kind of dirt out of me. I am sure Olivia couldn't keep her mouth shut after my mid-morning sexcapades yesterday. Especially when it looks like she is Daniel's newest target to stick his useless dick in.

"All business, no play makes for a boring life, Seven." His smug grin annoys me, but I will never let him know.

I throw him my megawatt smile and fire back. "Oh, Daniel. My life has a lot of play in it. I just keep it out of the office." Slam dunk. Well, it would be a slam dunk if it were actually true.

His feet drop to the floor, and he leans forward in the seat. "Not what I heard."

I let out a laugh. A deep, booming, belly laugh. I can't stop. I am absolutely hysterical and he looks at me as if I have lost the last bit of my sanity. I probably have. "Oh, Daniel. What I do in my personal time is none of your business. I suggest you keep your assumptions to yourself, because you don't have much of a leg to stand on." I love speaking cryptically. Never giving him too much information as to what I know, and what he thinks I know. It is all a game, and little does this bitch know, I am Milton fucking Bradley.

"I have nothing to hide, Seven. Which is why I still have my job here." He laughs at me. Wrong fucking move.

I snap.

"Daniel, everyone knows you can't keep that useless fucking dick in your pants. I know you're fucking my assistant. Everyone knows you cheat on your poor wife all the time. It's not news. But what I don't get is what these women see in you? Is it the money? Because you, my friend, are the worst fuck I have ever had. Every night when you would go back to your dorm room, I would finger myself, because you never once pleasured me the way a real man should."

Hey, I can't help that it's the truth. His ego is hurt for sure, and it makes me want to jump up and down while laughing in his face. But I sit still, composed behind my desk with a smile on my face. "Let me make something very clear, Daniel. Your time at Alexander Mobile is almost up. When the truth starts to leak out, you will be history. I suggest you step down before you cause your dear old daddy any embarrassment. Because that is all you are, a fucking embarrassment."

He is pissed. Like *really* fucking pissed off. If it were possible, steam would be spilling out of his ears. His face reddens, and his lips press together. He's searching for something witty to say, but nothing comes to him. I want to laugh at him some more, but I do us both a favor. "Enjoy your short time back at Alexander Mobile. Soon you will be gone. Now you can get out of my fucking office." I shoo him away with my hand.

"If you think it is going to be that easy to get rid of me, you are wrong, Seven." He stands in my doorway, trying to get the last word.

I shake my head and laugh at him. “Daniel, I don't think. I know.”

CHAPTER 11

Two Weeks Later

I walk into my penthouse to a familiar scene - Levi cooking up a storm in my kitchen. I'd be lying if I said I wasn't impressed by his cooking skills. Fuck, I'd be impressed with a bag of Ramen noodles and a bottle of beer, so when he pampers me with fancy dishes I could never hope to pronounce the name of, I don't complain at all.

"How did your meeting go?" I ask as I toss my laptop bag onto the kitchen counter, and slip out of my heels. I've been on the edge of my seat all day long waiting to hear how the alimony cookie would crumble. Levi and his lawyer sat down with his ex-gold digger, presenting her with all the information my wonderful PI had dug up on her affair with Daniel. She wouldn't get one more red cent from Levi.

"Very well. She was shocked, but I guess she knew it would be coming one day. My lawyer advised me that I could sue her for the spousal support I've been paying. I think I just want to be done with it all, though." He pulls two plates out of the cabinet above the sink and sets them down on the breakfast bar.

"Whatever you wanna do, Levi." I shrug as he fills our plates with some fancy pasta concoction that smells delicious. My mouth is watering, considering I haven't eaten a damn thing all day. My stomach lets out a deep growl, and we both laugh. The mood between us is always so light; we just mesh well in every sense.

"I wanted to talk to you about something." When those words leave his mouth, my body tenses. Those words are typically never good. Ever. Internally, I start to freak out. I should have known there would be trouble in paradise eventually.

The chip I had on my shoulder when I was trying to sidestep him all that time appears back in place. With an attitude I have no business throwing around, I jump down his throat. "What?"

"Relax, babe." He places the plate in front of me with a smile sprawling across his face. He really is gorgeous; everything from his stubble to the way his hair falls to the side does it for me, and I can't help but not be mad, or even irritated. "I put my penthouse on the market today." The words don't bother me.

"Whatever," I reply, completely oblivious to where the conversation is going.

"Seven, I put the penthouse on the market." His tone is more serious, and it draws my attention from the plate of pasta I am inhaling.

"Okay?" What does he want me to say? *Move in with me? Move into my home, which has doubled as a fuck pad for the duration of my residence?*

"How would you feel about buying a penthouse together?"

I drop my fork against the glass plate. It bounces off the dish and flies right onto the floor, pasta still attached and making a giant creamy mess. "What?" I ask him, my mouth gaping in his direction.

"Too much?" he asks. I don't even know how to answer that question, but my only internal reaction is to fucking run as far as I can. It was a big deal for me to agree to give him a *chance*. To give this whole thing a chance. We went from nothing to everything almost overnight. He's becoming my everything, and when he walks away, I'll be broken. I know this.

"Way too much, Levi." I let out a deep breath, and push the plate away from me. My appetite is gone now. "I can't do this. I need a break." I stand from my chair and start to back away from him. I need to put as much room between us as I can. If he touches me, I'll change my mind. "This is all too much, too fast. I need a break. Please, Levi. I hate to ask this of you, but can you go?" I can feel the panic attack brewing and I don't want him to witness the nastiness that is my manic behavior.

"Seven, can we please talk about this?" His tone is pleading, and I can't reply. I stand still, arms wrapped around my body, praying he'll walk out of my life as fast as he possibly can.

"Please. Go." My breathing becomes faster, and my hands shake as they harshly grip my own arms.

He turns without a word and makes his way to the elevator. Only a minute more and I can crack. Shatter. Retreat back into my fucked up head. Back to my fucked up life where I am worthless and where no one wants me. There, I am safe. The only person I am safe with is myself. It will always be like this.

I hear the slam of the elevator door and my entire body slips down the wall, sagging onto the kitchen floor as the hysterics pour out of me. First, it starts ever so slowly with tears. Followed by a meek cry. My breathing becomes more rapid with each memory that flashes through my overactive brain.

"You are destined to be alone, forever, Seven. You are just too fucked up." Blue's words echo through my ears.

"You'll never get your shit together long enough to love anyone but yourself," my father adds. Way to add insult to injury.

Without missing a beat, Daniel's voice slams through my ears.

"You are nothing more than a good fuck and a warm

body." He should have just carved my heart right out of my chest at that moment. "Seven, you aren't a forever kind of girl."

No, I am not built for forever. I am not the kind of girl you bring home to your parents. That had been drilled into my head repeatedly over the years. A good fuck, a warm body. But never a forever. My labored breaths turn into gasps for air, my shaking out of control as I sob uncontrollably on my kitchen floor. I am destined to be alone. Forever. That is the only forever I will get.

I lie on the floor for hours. Well, it seems like hours, but my panic attack lasts for only a few minutes. With my legs no longer feeling like Jell-O, I stand and make my way to the medicine cabinet in the bathroom, where I dig out a bottle of Xanax. I'll sleep tonight, but not because I'm comfortable in the arms of the only man I've ever truly loved. It will be because I'm too sedated to actually think about my fucked up life.

Ring ring, ring ring, ring ring, ring ring.

Stop fucking ringing already. Jesus fucking Christ. I don't want to be bothered. My cellphone continues ringing and vibrating until I can't take the racket anymore. Reaching over to the nightstand, I see Star's photo flashing on the display.

"Hello?" My voice is sedated, full of misery. It will be a miracle if she doesn't pick up on it.

"Seven? Are you okay?" Star whispers into the other end of the line.

I grunt, apparently now speaking caveman. "Yeah, I'm okay. How are you?" I try to turn this around on her. She has been gone for a while. Longer than I've ever spent away from her, except for college.

"I think I found the people who adopted her." I can hear her sniffle in the background; she's crying. "They died, years ago. There's no sign of Willow."

Fuck. Just what I needed on top of this whole fucked up situation. How can I even offer her kind words of comfort when I'm hurting just as bad? "It's okay, Star. I promise you, we will find her."

Her sobs grow quiet. "I hope so," she squeaks out.

"Keep in touch, Star. I gotta go back to bed."

I end the phone call. I can't listen to her tears without my own coming back. I want to be numb. Numb is exactly what I'm good at, although I wish I was better. I drift back off to sleep, only to be rudely awakened early by my fucking alarm screaming in my head as it pounds. Another day of work. Worst of all, I am going to have to deal with Levi *and* Daniel. Something I could honestly live without.

Two entire weeks have gone by. Two fucking weeks and I have done my best to ignore Levi. He has given me the space I need. He hasn't pressured me, only left sweet reminders of why I fell for him in the first place. Starting the morning after I asked him to leave.

I walked into my brightly lit office, and sitting in the center of my desk was a bright bouquet of colorful flowers. I smiled, even though I didn't want to. He was going to make this hard. Tossing my bag onto my chair, I snatched up the card attached to the flowers.

> *Seven,*
>
> *"She'll lie and steal and cheat. And beg you from her knees. Make you think she means it this time. She'll tear a hole in you, the one you can't repair. But I still love her, I don't really care. Don't leave me, Love. I don't think I can survive without you now.*

-Levi

A mixture of love and anger crashed over me. I picked the flowers up from my desk, chucking them across the room. Picking up the note from my desk, where it fell, I headed for Levi's office. I slammed the door open, and he sat behind his desk, just watching me.

I threw the card in his direction. "You can't do this to me. Please. Just let me go." I yelled; people looked and listened. He stood up and strode across the office, slamming the door behind me.

"Seven. I will not let you go." His body pressed me up against the door, his hard cock pressing against my stomach. I tried to push him off of me, but he was just too strong, and I was too exhausted from my lonely night. Drugged or not, I didn't sleep worth shit and I knew why. Because Levi wasn't in my bed.

I opened my mouth to speak and his lips crashed against mine. I tried to protest, but my body was such a fucking traitor. I gave in and kissed him back with everything I had. His fingers pushed my skirt farther up my legs, and I could feel him pushing my thong to the side. I moaned into his mouth as his tongue explored every corner of my mouth. He tasted like fresh toothpaste and mouthwash. Deliciously minty. Fuck!

As I pulled my mouth away to protest, I felt his thick cock press against my wet pussy. Before I could even object, he pushed in hard. "Fuck!" I breathed out, wrapping my legs around his waist. My body was on autopilot, and I was completely helpless when it came to anything that had to do with him. His length rubbed against my clit as he pushed into me roughly.

"Seven. I can't live without this," he whispered into my ear. I tried to block out everything going on and just feel his dick inside me. Deeper than I think he has ever been.

My orgasm crashed over me, as his hand pressed against

my mouth, muffling the screams. His come flooded into me a moment later. His grip loosened, and my legs slid back down to the floor, barely holding me up. Pants somewhere around his ankles, he turned to walk away from me, completely ignoring everything that had just happened between us. I pushed my skirt down and turned for the door. I felt used, which was a first. In all the years of my meaningless sex, I had never once felt used.

Out of the corner of my eye, I saw him pulling his pants up, and I ran out the door, stalking toward the safety of my office as fast as I could. Once I was inside, I slammed the door closed and prayed no one noticed what had just happened. Fucking office gossip. I needed a damn vacation.

I make it through the rest of that day trying not to think about Levi. Which is hard because work has started to slow down. Soon enough, I won't be in the office at Alexander Mobile daily, and I can retreat back to my old building, far from Levi and Daniel's fucking nosy ass.

It would be really fucking nice if Star was home right now. I can't help but miss her. I've been lying through my teeth every time she calls. I won't let her know Levi and I are over, because she'll turn her ass around and high tail it right back to the city. She needs to be looking for her little girl. There will never be any peace in her life until she finds Willow. My heart breaks for her, repeatedly. The idea of becoming a mother has never been something I was fond of. Even under the shitty circumstances, though, Star brought that little girl into the world, and I find myself jealous. She has the opportunity to have someone who will love and want her for the rest of her life.

Had she been given the chance, she would have never let that little girl go. I know that for a damn fact. The situation makes me hate my family even more, and hers to boot.

Realizing I've been lost in my head for damn near an hour, I make my way home for the day. My evening will be identical to what it's been since the night I asked Levi to leave.

Shitty takeout food, longing for something homemade by Levi. A long bubble bath, praying he will appear in the tub with me. Followed by a sleepless night, tossing and turning with nightmares about the past and the future. Will I ever be at peace again?

CHAPTER 12

Three Days Later

The week sucked, and the weekend got even worse. The food poisoning I got Friday night lasted all weekend long. At least, I think it's food poisoning, but it certainly seems like the fucking plague. Every time my head hits the plush pillows on my bed, my stomach rolls, the room starts spinning, and I launch myself in the direction of the bathroom. A handful of times I didn't even make it to the fucking toilet. Leaving me to clean up vomit, splattered all over the marble. Just what I wanted to do when I was nauseous.

Sleep has been virtually non-existent, except for when I finally pass out. My body can't take any more of the dry heaves, and it simply shuts down. I'm grateful for that, until the nightmares start. It's a vicious cycle. I jolt awake only to be greeted by whatever is left in my stomach making an escape. Just when I think I am going to die, alone in my apartment from tainted Thai food, there's a light at the end of the tunnel.

Sunday afternoon, I wake from one of my stretches of sleep, induced by being absolutely exhausted, and finally start to feel human again. I have something to be happy about for the first time in weeks, getting the fuck out of bed without hurling. I take a nice long shower and brush my teeth, and I feel like a million bucks. Until I think about Levi.

Being so fucking sick, I haven't had time to think about the shitty situation I've found myself in with Levi. I haven't been able to think about how much I miss him, or how much I wish he was here, in my penthouse with me, holding my hair back as I yack. It's not a perfect happily ever after, but it's something I want, with him. I want a life with Levi..

Against my better judgment, I text him. I miss him. I want him. I've been fucking stupid to think I could walk away from the only person who ever truly wanted me.

Hey.

It's not much, but for the first time since I sent him packing, it's me contacting him. My phone quickly vibrates, indicating his reply. Was he sitting on top of the phone waiting for me?

Hey?

Don't sound so happy to hear from me. God. Maybe it's too late.

What's new?

Apparently, I am turning into an awkward high school girl. Soon I'll be using LOL and giggling too. Yup, I have officially lost it. I am beyond desperate.

Missing you. What's new with you?

Relief floods through my body. He misses me. I miss him. Shouldn't this be a lot easier, and far less nerve-wracking than it is?

I miss you too. Come over?

Will I live to regret those words? Probably, but the only thing I need at this moment is Levi. Inside me, holding me, kissing me. I need everything about him. I've needed him all weekend long, as I laid on the cold tile in my bathroom re-enacting *The Exorcist* the best I could. Linda Blair would have fucking been impressed, that is for sure.

You sure?

Am I sure? No. But I have never really been sure about anything in my life. Even when I think I'm sure, I end up making a shitty decision that sends my life into a mother fucking tailspin. My own judgment should never be trusted when it comes to my personal life.

I can make business decisions like a boss. My personal life? Not so much.

Yes. I miss you. I need you.

I shouldn't have admitted that last part, but I guess this will be the first step toward admitting I never really needed space to begin with. I've been stupid all along.

Be there shortly.

My heart flutters at the thought of him. This whole emotional roller-coaster called love has really fucked me all up. Do I really love him? Could I walk away so easily if I did? My mind is a giant cluster-fuck of feelings and thoughts that I would have never expected in a fucking million years.

I pick up my phone to text him one last time before he

arrives.

Can't wait.

It is the God's honest truth. I can't wait to see him. We have skirted around each other every chance that we've had, after the morning I threw the vase of flowers across his office and he fucked me against the door. If this is love, it's fucked up. But with me, fucked up seems to be the only kind of way I roll through life.

The elevator doors open as I walk out of the kitchen with a glass of ginger ale in my hands. I still look like I've been hit by a fucking truck. My hair is thrown up in a messy knot on the top of my head, my nail polish is chipped, and I've been picking at it for days. I have on a pair of giant grey sweatpants I could fit a family of five inside, and my black I Love Haters t-shirt hugs my braless tits. There's nothing beautiful about the dark circles around my eyes, either.

I look up, and our eyes meet across the foyer. Levi starts heading toward me; he looks perfect. His hair is gelled back, and he wears a snug fitting pair of jeans and a white button down shirt, with the sleeves rolled up. Casual, but so fucking sexy. His face quickly changes from ecstatic to see me to concerned as he walks closer.

"Seven, what the fuck is wrong?" His arms wrap around my aching body, his fingers caress the side of my face, and I can see the look of genuine worry in his eyes. He cares. As much as I've wanted to tell myself that this isn't meant to be, that he doesn't really want me, he cares a whole hell of a lot.

"Got food poisoning. But I'm feeling better."

He lets out a sigh and pulls me up into his arms. "You should have texted me sooner; I should have been here taking care of you all weekend." Holding me tight in his arms, he brings me to my bedroom, where he lays me down on the bed, so damn gently.

He doesn't want to break me, and the consideration is downright adorable. I can't help but swoon over this man; he is damn near perfect.

“How are you feeling now?” He runs his finger along the outline of my face.

“Eh, somewhat human, I guess.”

He moves closer, lying next to me, never taking his gorgeous eyes off of me. “What do you want to do?” he asks me, and all I want to do is have him hold me all night. Make love to me. Come home to my body, and never leave my side again, no matter how much I demand it.

“I'm sorry, Levi. I should have never let you walk out that door. I'm just... I'm fucked up.” I want to open up; I want to explain everything to him, but I just don't even know where to start. I tried to cover it in London, but I knew in the back of my mind that I'd left so much out. That landed me right here, smack dab in the middle of the mess that I created, yet again.

My story is so fucking long, and downright crazy. “No one has ever wanted me. Not my parents. Not my brother. Not the one person I ever found myself in a relationship with. No one but Star, and even that is questionable.” *We have to be honest here. Friendship or not, she has been a shitty friend on occasion.*

“It's how I *try* to protect myself from getting hurt. Pushing the people who care away. To me? This was all too good to be true. I never thought I would want the whole happily ever after, but then you came along and screwed my whole head up.” I can't help but laugh at the conversation I find myself in. “Levi, my feelings for you scared me so much I needed to get away. I couldn't breathe. My whole world is upside down.”

He watches me attentively, carefully taking in each word I say. He listens, and listens until there's nothing left for me to say. By this point, I should feel a panic attack brewing. Instead, a wave of nausea hits me again.

I jump from the bed, scrambling for the bathroom and

kicking the door closed on my way. Up comes the small glass of ginger ale I thought I'd be able to keep down. Fuck! Maybe this is the flu, because if it's dinner two nights ago causing this bullshit, I am going to own that fucking Thai place.

A soft knock sounds from the door. The knob turns and Levi stands there, watching me with pity in his eyes. He looks as helpless as I feel. "You okay?" he asks.

I want to throw him one of my typical witty comebacks about being just fucking dandy, but I can't open my mouth. I know if I try to speak, another round of gagging is going to commence.

I nod in his direction. He opens the cabinet on the far side of the bathroom and wets a washcloth. He brings it over and gently places it on the back of my neck, before he starts rubbing my back. I am the luckiest girl on Earth. I swear.

I grab the washcloth and wipe my face and mouth, before tossing it to the side. I stand on shaky feet, and head for the sink to scrub the vomit from my mouth for the gazillionth time this weekend. In the bedroom, I hear the alarm sounding on my phone, screeching through the quiet of my penthouse.

"What the hell is that?" Levi listens, and follows the noise until he finds my iPhone laying on the floor next to my bed. He holds it up, reading the screen. "Birth control alarm?" He smirks, but panic starts coursing through my veins.

Holy fucking shit. It can't fucking be. There is no fucking way. Please God! Fucking no!

I start to mentally count back to the last period I had. Two, three, four, five… *Oh shit. No.* This isn't fucking good at all. London. Time change. Same fucking alarm time. Pills at the wrong time. Not the same time every damn day like I have religiously managed for as long as I can remember. I fucked up so fucking bad.

It's like my worst nightmare coming true. Just days ago, I was thinking about how lucky Star is, always having someone who will love her, and want her, and now I find myself in the same fucking position. All I want to do is run to the closest abortion clinic I can find.

There is no fucking way in the world I can tell Levi. By the look on his face, I don't need to tell him; he already knows. My face shows the sheer panic; looking up in the mirror, I'm pale as hell.

"Seven, are you okay?"

My eyes grow wide with panic. I can't look him in the eye. He walks across the room, handing me my phone. His arms wrap around me, and he holds me tight. I bury my face into his chest and start crying. Not crying because I'm angry, or upset. I'm crying because I have no idea what I am going to do.

"It's okay, Seven," he whispers into my ear while he rubs my back. "It is okay. I am not going anywhere."

"London. It happened in London, Levi. The time change screwed my pills up. I took them at the wrong time. I fucked up." I get the words out in between my sobs. "I am so sorry."

Two hours and a box of pregnancy tests later, it's confirmed. I'm pregnant. Levi knocked me up and I have no idea what the fuck I am going to do. My initial thought is to book an appointment at the local abortion clinic, and make sure this never happens again. Ever. I might as well book an appointment to have my tubes tied as well.

Levi's words break my thoughts. "Seven? What do you want to do?"

The question is so innocent, but it's so fucking loaded. I don't even know how to answer it, because I never thought I'd find myself in a situation like this. Hell, all the sex I've had over the years. Not only have I been on top of my trusty birth control pill, but I never, ever, didn't use a condom. Until Levi. Does this fucking guy have super sperm or is my luck just that fucking bad?

I pause, my mind racing, but I don't answer his question. How do you tell a man you are trying to repair your broken relationship with that the only option in your mind is to run, not walk, to an abortion clinic, and kill your baby? Yup, nothing unexpected. I am just fucked up like that.

"Levi, I..." A single tear rolls down my cheek, which he quickly brushes away with his finger. "I want an abortion." The words sting. They feel like poison coming out of my mouth, but that isn't even the worst part of it. The look on Levi's face is enough to send me to my grave. My heart is broken, again. I have hurt him, again. I can't help but hurt him over and over. He would be so much better off without me.

He pulls me tight against his body, rubbing his hand along my back.

"Seven." I can hear the words he wants to say choked back in his throat. He is going to cry, and if he does, I will completely lose the last bit of calm I have. "Are you... sure?"

I want to say no, I want to say that I am not sure. I wish I could just accept it, and be happy like any other woman would be. But we all know I am just fucked up beyond your average woman.

"No, I am not sure, Levi. What do you want?"

That came out of left field. I shouldn't care what he wants, but I do. I shouldn't want that happily ever after with him. But I do. I shouldn't want kids and marriage and all that foo foo bullshit. But I do. I fucking want it all. I want everything I never had a single desire for. But it isn't until Levi opens his mouth and answers me that I make my decision.

"Seven, I can't make you do anything. If you want to have an abortion, that is your choice. And I will support you. I will support you in anything you do, because I love you." *He loves me?*

"But I can't say I want you to have an abortion, because I don't. I want you. I want a baby with you. I want you in my life forever."

He pauses, and squeezes me tighter against his body, before he nervously runs his ringers through his now messy hair. "The very thought of you pregnant, with my baby, does something to me. God, Seven. It turns me on. Thinking about you with that sexy round belly, full with my baby."

I feel his hard cock pressing against my ass as he cradles me in his arms. His words shouldn't change my mind, but they do. A few minutes ago, an abortion was the only option in my mind, and now, the possibility of a happily ever after is right in front of my face. I want to jump and take it. I want to grab the American Dream by the horns and make it my bitch.

The reality of it all, though, is that I need a couple days to think about it. I can't make such a life changing choice in only a few minutes. I need to talk to Star. I need to let it settle. The businesswoman in me rears her ugly head, and I know a decision so big can't be made with hasty choices, because Levi and I still don't know each other. It's new. It may not work out. And if it doesn't, I don't want our lives to play out like an episode of *Jerry Springer.*

"Levi? What if it doesn't work out? With us?" Since when have I become so open with communication? Maybe this is just a new and improved Seven. The Seven that has been begging to come out since she was an unwanted little girl.

"I can't tell the future, Seven. I'm not going to pretend like everything is going to be sunshine and kittens, because life sucks sometimes. I figured that out these past weeks when I was forced to live without you. But one thing I can tell you is that I don't want a life without you. I don't want to even think about it. Sure, this is unplanned. Sure, most couples get a long time together before a child comes into the world. But this is the card we have been handed. This is our love story. Who are we to question fate?"

Fate.

Is this our fate?

With the shock and nausea behind me, I'm starting to feel somewhat better by bedtime. Levi ran out to the corner store and stocked up on Saltine crackers and ginger ale. They're the only two things that I can keep down. Well, for short periods of time anyway.

I call my doctor and make an appointment for first thing in the morning, meaning I will take my first day off from work in almost two years. If I'm going to survive being pregnant and continue to dominate the world, I need some kind of fancy medication to keep me from emptying the contents of my stomach several times a day.

Most of all, I need this pregnancy to remain hidden as long as possible, at least at work. I'm just not ready for the rumor mill to start churning, and honestly, after my flower throwing scene, everyone will immediately know this has something to do with Levi. Sitting on a board with your baby mama isn't the ideal situation.

I curl up next to his warm body wearing nothing but an oversized t-shirt. I am trying desperately to get comfortable as his arm wraps around my waist. His fingers snake up my shirt and rest gently against the warm skin of my flat stomach. The intimate touch slowly drives out any reservations I have about my choice.

Sometimes in life, you have to throw caution to the wind. You have to take a chance on something that may not be a sure thing. This is what we call living. It isn't fair to tread through life calculating the repercussions of every move. Simply existing isn't for me anymore. I am going to take a risk. Take a chance. I am going to give myself to Levi, and if my world comes crashing down, it won't be the fucking first time, and I know it very well won't be the last. Not by a long shot.

I cannot, and will not, run from life anymore.

His fingers run across my tattooed stomach, not leaving an inch untouched by his loving caress. I roll over and face him. We just stare into each other's eyes. We have an entire conversation without speaking a single word. I can see the genuine love in his eyes, and just like the damn Grinch, my heart grows three sizes in that moment. I lean in and brush my lips against his.

Pulling away, I speak.

"Levi, make love to me."

His hand runs up my body, moving along my face, and his fingers thrust through my hair. "There is nothing I would rather do right now."

And for the first time in a long time, if ever, we make love.

Levi rises to his knees, hovering over my body, and gently pulls the oversized t-shirt over my head. I hook my fingers in the waistband of his boxer-briefs and slide them down his legs as our mouths meet in sweet seductive kisses. His tongue runs along my bottom lip, and when my lips part to let out a quiet moan of anticipation, he pushes into my mouth. We make out like virgins waiting for their wedding night, while lying naked in each other's arms. His hand cups my chin, and his kisses start to drag down my body.

He stops to show my pebbled nipples extra attention. The sensations send shockwaves through my body, and the only thing I want is his dick deep inside me. His mouth sucks on one nipple, and then the other, as I beg for more.

"Levi, please! I need you inside me."

But he continues his lazy way down my aching body, not leaving an inch untouched.

When he reaches my stomach, he spends extra time kissing, caressing, and he stops to lay his head down for a moment. He stills before he whispers, "I love you," and continues his downward journey to my center.

His fingers find my wet pussy and slowly make their entry as he lowers his mouth and gently sucks on my clit. My body explodes at his touch.

"Levi! Fuck!" I can't help but scream out in pleasure as he continues lapping up all the juices my body generously gives to him. His mouth leaves my center, and his lips crash against my mouth. The taste of my sweet orgasm is all over his face.

"You are beautiful when you come." Yup. This man is going to kill me tonight.

I feel his hardness press against my waiting cunt; I am so wet and ready to take him. I lift my hips, begging him to push into me. A smile spreads across his face - his beautiful, sculpted, manly face. A face that I am coming to realize I absolutely fucking love. His dick slowly pushes inside my pussy. I can feel the walls stretching to accommodate his glorious size. Inch-by-inch, he slowly enters until I feel his balls meet my ass. When he is all the way in, I wrap my legs around his waist, and I pull him closer, wrapping my arms around his neck and locking his mouth in a passionate kiss. With each tender tease and bite, I show him just how much he means to me.

He slowly starts to pull out, only to push back in with lazy thrusts. In and out, slow but so damn good. I can feel every inch of his cock claiming me. My second orgasm starts to build as the tip of his dick starts brushing my g-spot. His eyes never move from mine, silently showering me with unspoken worship. A tear slips down my cheek, and he leans in to kiss it away. His thumb grazes my swollen clit and my release crashes over me. I moan quietly, as he lets out his final grunts, spilling deep inside me.

No sooner then he is done, my stomach flip-flops and I run for the bathroom. I can only hope this whole morning sickness thing is fucking gone soon, because nine months of this shit is not going to fly.

CHAPTER 13

My Day Off

Two years, two damn years since I have had to call out of work. I got lucky, scoring a late morning appointment with my OB/GYN. If she wanted me there for nine in the morning, I may have been tattooing the waiting room with whatever I had left in my stomach. All night, and first thing this morning, Levi held my hair back, rubbed my back, and became my own personal waitress, pacing back and forth from the kitchen to the master bedroom with anything I thought I wanted.

Bottles of water, ginger ale, crackers, wet washclothes. I think I even started to beg for shots of whiskey at one point before he talked me down. Once eleven rolled around, and he had been off at the office for roughly two hours, I had Clyde drive me across town for my appointment. There was already enough speculation flying around the office; we didn't want to add more.

It's been about six months since I've been here, checking in for my annual exam, one of the fucking best parts of being a woman. I didn't think I'd be here until next June sometime.

"Seven James, eleven-twenty appointment." The girl behind the desk scans her computer screen, grabs a clipboard, and hands me the pile of paperwork. “We are going to need a urine sample as well,” she says and places a small sterile cup on top of the clipboard. Wonder how much of the pee I will actually get inside the cup instead of on my hand? Story of my life.

My stomach spins and I take a deep breath, trying to breathe through the wave of nausea. *Man, this blows.* I take a seat in the black plastic waiting room chair, and dive into the stack of papers. Question after question about my periods, family health history, birth defects, and more shit I have no idea of. Nor will I be calling my parents to ask. I could imagine how that would go over. *Hi, Mom? Yeah, I am knocked up by some guy I just met and I need to know if anyone in our family has had any sort of a birth defect?* Um. No.

My phone buzzes in my pocket. I start digging through the death trap I call a purse and locate it among my eyeliner and the brush I carry around. Star's bright face lights up the screen, and I quietly answer it, despite the huge no cellphone sign sitting across the waiting room.

“Hey, I can't talk. Can I call you back in an hour?”

She quickly agrees, although I can tell she is bursting at the seams with some kind of news. I can only hope it is actually good news for once. After all the dead ends in her search for Willow, I wish I could help more.

“Seven James?” A woman in pink scrubs appears in the doorway, smiling, with a manila folder in her hands. But it’s the blonde holding onto a small crying baby that catches my attention.

“Seven?” Samantha turns in my direction. Samantha Alexander, Daniel's poor wife. “Oh my goodness! How are you?” Her tone is fake, as the little bundle of blue on her shoulder cries. She bounces her step, and pats him on his back. “Shhhhh, Danny, it’s okay, baby,” she coos to him.

“It was nice seeing you, Samantha,” I say and run in the direction of the bathroom as my sad attempt at a cracker-based breakfast makes its way back up my throat. *Might as well pee in the cup while I'm at it.*

"Sample," I say holding the cup out to the poor nurse. "Sorry about that. I can't stop throwing up for the life of me."

As the words leave my mouth, I see another woman in scrubs escorting Samantha through the door to the exam rooms. Her curious gaze falls on me, and surely she has heard exactly what I just said. It won't be long until the entire world knows I was throwing up in the OB/GYN's office, because that is just the kind of person she is. Hell, I would be absolutely shocked if she hasn't texted Daniel my exact location already. *Fuck!*

"Right this way." The room is cold, and sterile. But this time of year, everything is fucking freezing in New York City. "I am going to need you to strip from the waist down and wait for the doctor." She turns and walks out of the room, allowing me privacy to strip. *Jeez, they could have at least bought me dinner first.*

I sit on the table, thumbing over Candy Crush and trying to pass the time until the doctor finally makes her appearance in the ice box of an exam room. My phone indicates a text message, and I open it up. Of course, it is from Levi.

> **How are you feeling? Board meeting went bad this morning. Will be home early this afternoon. If you need anything on my way, text.**

Of course it went bad; those asshats can't do anything right without me breathing down their necks. I am sure that the fact that I took a single day off sent half the office into a tailspin.

> **I'm okay. Waiting to see the doctor. Text you after my appointment.**

The door slowly opens. "Miss James?" the doctor says, questioning if I am decent.

"Come on in."

The next half hour goes by in a blur of medical questions, and ends with me begging for some kind of medication to calm my stomach, allowing me to get through a full day of work without announcing to the entire corporate sector that I am with child. I score a prescription for some high priced fancy nausea medication called Zofran, which is supposed to be heaven sent for those women barely surviving their first trimester, like myself.

But it isn't until the doctor pulls a little machine over and asks me to lay back and spread 'em that I start to worry. Especially when the machine comes attached with a wand that looks like the vibrator I keep in my toy closet.

"And that is for?" I question, and he lets out an uncomfortable laugh.

"I am going to do an ultrasound. Oh, and I have to order a round of blood work. But you don't have to have that done today. Just make sure you have that prescription filled; the sooner you start taking it, the sooner you will be able to function better.

"This may be a little uncomfortable for a minute."

He slides the wand inside my very unfriendly vagina, and starts clicking away on the screen. "Looks like you are about five weeks. That little flicker there is the heartbeat. It is too soon to hear it, but it looks pretty strong for five weeks. These dates are only estimates though."

A little printer spits out a small black and white photo that looks something like a blob. There are no arms or legs. No viable head or extremities. It doesn't look like much of anything, but knowing it is alive, inside of me, makes me almost sick that my initial thought was abortion. Not even twenty four hours after finding out, I am in full on protective mama bear mode.

"Come back in about two weeks, and we will try to get a listen to the heartbeat." He smiles, and hands me the prescription, and the photo. "Don't forget to get the blood work done." Like that, he is gone.

I hold onto the prescription, and run my thumb over the

printed photo. A smile pulls at my lips, just in time for me to dry heave into the garbage can next to the exam table.

The phone rings and rings until a breathless Star finally picks up. “Star? Is everything all right?”

She pauses on the other end of the line, before speaking. “Yes! Seven! I found her! I think, I think I found her!” She doesn't give very many details, but she goes on about a farmer on the edge of town in Woodstock, something about a brother's cousin or nephew who had a little girl around Willow's age. A long story about her parents being killed in a car accident when she was young. Living with family. She gushes about it before stopping to ask me how things in the city are going.

“Well, Star. Are you sitting down?” I have to laugh, because I never thought I would be the one dishing this kind of news to her. In fact, I couldn't say I was completely surprised when she told me she had a child, because I always pegged her as getting knocked up first. Technically, I guess she did accomplish that before I did.

“Are you okay, Seven?”

“Depends on what you consider okay? I will live, but this baby growing inside me isn't letting me keep a single fucking thing down. I have been puking my guts out for days.”

I hear an audible gasp on the other end of the line. She is silent for a minute before she starts giggling like a little girl. “Please say it is Levi's!”

“Of course it is Levi's! But I am not telling anyone, especially my fucking family. So keep your loud mouth shut!” The town car pulls up to my building. “I gotta run, Star, but when you come home, we will catch up. I hope you find her. Soon."

Like that, Star is gone and I am on my way up to the penthouse, in serious need of some ginger ale and a fucking nap. But only after I text Levi and let him know everything is okay, and I need for him to pick up my prescription on his way to the penthouse later.

Everything went well. Can you pick up my prescription on your way here?

I throw down all the stuff in my arms on the little coffee table next to the couch. Ultrasound picture, cellphone, keys, and purse. My phone vibrates, and Levi has replied.

No problem. Text me the pharmacy. I will be on my way as soon as I can.

I can't help but smile at how fortunate I am. He really is amazing.

Sipping on my bubbly soda, which for once seems to be helping my stomach, I lie down on the couch and close my eyes. What seems like a few minutes must have been hours, and I'm woken by the elevator opening into the foyer of my penthouse.

"Levi, baby. Finally," I groan, not making a move to get off the couch.

I hear footsteps, but he doesn't speak. I slowly roll over, blinking my eyes open, but Levi isn't the one standing in my living room. Daniel is, and now I am not only wide awake, but I am pretty fucking pissed that he is standing in my house.

"Hoping to see someone else?" he asks with a smirk on his face.

"Well, I can't say I invited you here. I am out of the office for a reason today," I sass him back with attitude. He is the last person I feel like dealing with.

"Oh, I know. Samantha called me as soon as she saw you. Seven James, finally knocked up after all these years. I must admit, I thought it would have happened long ago."

I flip him the bird, and sit up on the couch. I am exhausted. My whole body feels like it is still sleeping, and I can barely move.

"It's none of your fucking business, Daniel. I suggest you leave, before I fucking call the cops."

His expression darkens, and this is the first time in my entire life that I have actually been scared of a man. Never would I have imagined Daniel causing this kind of a feeling.

"First you storm into my fucking office, and steal my company from under my nose." He steps closer to the couch and pauses again. "Then that fucking little bitch Parker was married to fucked up the money coming into my pocket when some PI found the traces of our affair." His hands run through his barely there hair, and he fucking growls. Like a fucking dog. Growls.

I try and stand up, but he pushes me back down with so much force that my head hits the back of the couch. My stomach churns and I can feel the bile rising up my throat. It isn't going to be long before I start throwing up the soda I thought was safe in my stomach.

I reach for my phone and he forcefully grabs my wrist. Tight. And it fucking hurts. Like really fucking hurts. I can see a bruise appearing under his grip as he continues to tighten his grip, and I can't make it to my fucking cellphone.

"Is this your little bastard? Is it Parker's? You know that baby his wife shit out? That was mine, too. Too bad this one isn't mine. If I had gotten to you sooner, it could have been. You would have liked to have my baby, right, Seven?"

He releases my wrist and throws it into my lap. I try to stand again, and he shoves me with the palm of his hand. The wind is knocked out of me and I gasp for air. My head hits the pillow on the couch as I clench my chest. From the corner of my eye, I see him pulling at his belt. Next comes his button and finally, his zipper.

I'm frozen against the couch, trying to catch my breath. I try and move again, and I feel his hand grip my throat. Fuck. I am going to die like this. At the hands of Daniel, in my own living room. I can't hold back the vomit any longer. I turn my head to the side and throw up all over the floor. He lets go of my throat, and I can feel his hands tugging on my pants.

"Seven, you will never belong to anyone else. This pussy, no matter how slutty you are now, will always belong to me. Do you understand me? ME! It was mine first. Say it, Seven, say I had you first. Tell me how it felt when I took your virginity."

My pants come loose just as the elevator doors open. I can tell the sound anywhere, but Daniel is too preoccupied with taking what he thinks is his. Tears roll down my cheeks until I can see Levi in my line of vision.

"What the FUCK is going on here?"

Daniel turns toward Levi, cool as a fucking cucumber and tries to play it off. "Sorry you have to find out like this, Parker, but she has been mine for years." He lets out a laugh. What he doesn't count on is the fact that I have enough adrenaline coursing through my veins to finally get up off the couch. I pick up my purse and swing it through the air like it's filled with bricks. One solid hit and Daniel loses his footing, stumbling forward toward Levi. That is when Levi's fist connects with Daniel's face, and he falls, out-cold onto the floor.

I am in full blown hysterics by now, crying my eyes out. I can't even think about what almost just happened. Daniel almost raped me. Daniel almost hurt me. But Levi saved me.

If there was any ounce of doubt left, it's gone. This man loves me. He would do anything for me. He saved me.

Levi wraps his arms around me, trying to calm me down as he calls the police. Twenty or so minutes later, my foyer is full of NYPD officers whom I have no desire to speak with.

CHAPTER 14

The Aftermath of Daniel Alexander
(Two Weeks Later)

I'd be a liar if I said I didn't feel some sort of pity for Daniel Alexander. The boy was born and bred into the world of business, only to flop like a fish out of water. With his mother's history of slipping mental health, I'm not surprised the apple fell so close to the tree.

It turns out Daniel had a half dozen kids, with a half dozen women. Three with his actual wife, one with Levi's ex-wife and another on the way with her, and one with a teenage prostitute, whom he was supporting with company money. How he thought the company would never find out about his shady dealings is beyond me. The attempted assault was just the icing on his felony cake. Between money laundering, theft, insider trading, and the nice attempted rape charge, Alexander Mobile's golden boy will be sharing a scummy prison cell with some guy named Bubba for the next thirty or so years. Karma genuinely is a bitch.

I do feel bad for the women he's duped. Well, except for Levi's ex-wife; she knew exactly what she was getting into when she got involved with him so many years ago.

I lucked out. Had Levi not gotten home from the office when he did, I cannot imagine what would have happened. I hate to admit it, but even during the years that I dated Daniel, I never saw him mad. The crazy look in his eyes told me something was, in fact, very wrong.

I shake my head, trying to forget it all. I just want to forget altogether. Looking down, I smile at the newly framed photo on my desk. She is a beautiful little girl, with bright blue eyes that could light up the entire city of Manhattan on a gloomy night. Her long blond hair hangs in braided pigtails down to her waist, and her beautiful mother, my best friend, Star holds her, with a matching smile.

It may not be the ideal situation, but Star was able to meet and spend time with her daughter, who is turning eleven in a few short weeks. She begged Chrome, Willow's adoptive father, to bring her to the city for Christmas, and for her birthday, but the jury was still out. *Who comes up with these fucking names anyway? Chrome? Is his brother named Spoke? What about a sister named Sissy Bar? Fucking bikers.*

And today… Well, today is my second doctor's appointment. Today, Levi and I will be able to listen to our baby's heartbeat.

Levi is already the epitome of a good dad. He cleaned Barnes & Noble out of their entire pregnancy section. I could probably buy Dr. Sears himself and Levi wouldn't be content. I won't tell him, but it is fucking adorable, even if it annoys the living shit out of me. I totally feel human again, too. The medication my doctor prescribed has worked wonders. Absolute fucking wonders. I mean, don't get me wrong, I still barf daily, but it is way less than before, and I can actually keep a meal down.

"You ready?" I hear Levi open my office door; he peeks in. I wave him off and continue typing. I'm wrapping up the last email on my agenda before we take off to Vegas for a long weekend.

"One more minute, then I am yours until Tuesday. Well, after the appointment." I send off the email, and close my laptop, sliding it into my bag.

"Let me take that." He's concerned, not wanting me to carry more than my tits.

"A laptop isn't going to kill me, Levi." I roll my eyes, and he shrugs. The battle has been lost. "I was thinking we can add a couple things to the *before baby* list once we get in the air."

I laugh. Yes, there you have it, folks; we have become that cheesy couple. We have a list of shit to do before the baby comes. But unlike your typical suckers, *paint the nursery* and *buy a sedan* aren't anywhere to be found.

"I can't start thinking about the *before baby* list right now, Seven. We will never make it to the appointment, and I don't want to miss this one." He wraps his arms around my waist and pulls me in for a lingering kiss. I can feel his erection pressing against my stomach, and I know he is as worked up about the list as I am.

"But what if I want to be late?" My hand inches down his body, stroking his bulge.

His lips nip at my earlobe, driving me absolutely wild. "Mile high club?"

The three word promise is enough to hold me over, until we are in the air in a few hours. But God, I still want him right this damn second… Fuck!

"Miss James, come on back." The same nurse as my last visit escorts me to the bathroom, asking for more pee, then insists I step on a scale.

"You. Turn the other way." I point at Levi, and he laughs

and turns to face away from the display on the scale.

"You didn't lose any weight; that is great!" The nurse is over the moon. I guess she really takes her job seriously. She leaves us alone in the room, waiting for the doctor. Levi thumbs over some brochures on the counter, and I tap my finger nervously against the metal side of the exam table. "You should have seen it last time. I was half naked and the doctor came at me with that wand thing. I can't even laugh about where he shoved it." I point at the wand on the ultrasound machine sitting across from me. That shit is totally taunting me too, laughing at my fear.

A knock comes, and the doctor makes his way in. "Nice to see you again, Miss James, and Mr..." He trails off, extending his hand to Levi.

"Parker, Levi Parker," he replies in greeting.

"They should have asked you to strip from the waist down, Miss James. We are going to do another ultrasound." Dread runs across my face, and Levi looks like he wants to burst out laughing. *Real fucking funny. Why don't I probe YOU with that? Never mind, I am sure you would like it.*

"I thought we were just going to hear the heartbeat today?" My question is genuine, and I am totally trying to get out of the vaginal probe again; wouldn't you be?

"Seven, it is still too early to hear it from the outside of your stomach. We have to do an internal ultrasound again."

I stop complaining when I see Levi's entire face light up like a Christmas tree. He's excited and, even though I am downright miserable, his gleeful expression makes me willing to walk to Hell and back with that stupid wand up my vag just to keep that smile plastered on his face. I am so losing my fucking edge.

The doctor leaves, only long enough for me to slide down the black pinstriped slacks I have on, and climb back onto the exam table. Levi scoots the chair closer to my side and takes a hold of my hand. He kisses the tip of each finger, and stops when his lips press to the back of my hand. "I can't wait to see our baby," he quietly says, as the door opens back up.

"We ready?"

The doctor starts typing on the ultrasound machine again, and I can't do anything but let out a sigh. "Yes." The probe does its thing. This time it isn't all bad. I guess my nerves last time around made shit like a million times worse. I'm a regular old pro now.

"Is that…" Levi trails off, looking at the screen, still holding tightly onto my hand.

"Sure is. Your baby. Let me track down the heartbeat." The doctor moves the wand, and we can both see it squirming around. It isn't much, but you can see the distinct movements on the screen. To the right, then a little bit to the left. Then the most wonderful sound fills my ears.

Woosh, woosh, woosh, woosh, woosh, woosh, woosh, woosh.

"That is the heartbeat, nice and strong. I will print out a couple more pictures as well." He continues doing whatever it is doctors do with these machines, and I look at Levi, completely stunned and trying not to cry. These damn hormones have me crying more than I have in my entire life. Literally.

Any reservations about having a baby are gone. The idea that I almost opted for an abortion runs through my mind on repeat, but I know in my heart, I could have never gone through with it. If it had been anyone else other than Levi by my side for this, I would have hightailed it over to the abortion clinic without a second thought, but this man just makes my world so worth living once again. I have been on autopilot for so many years, just getting by day-to-day, and then he walked into my life. My kink club. I used him as a play thing. He used me as his Dom. The universe just couldn't let it be, though, and I am glad. It was time for me to actually live. Be wanted. Stop living in the past. This is my future. Levi, and this baby. Fuck, it looks bright.

"You know we are only going for a three night vacation, right, Seven?" Levi laughs as he helps Clyde pull the bags out of the car. I wave him off and walk up the stairs to the private jet, sitting on the tarmac.

"I pay him to do that, you know that, right?"

He ignores me and continues helping my damn hired help, and I make myself comfortable.

I pop a Dramamine, and my nausea medication with the bottle of ginger ale, which I now carry in my purse everywhere I go. People who tell you it doesn't work are liars. It helps immensely. Levi sits down next to me as I pick up my notebook and pull out the list. "I believe we have some work to do.

The Before Baby List

Join the Mile High Club
One last threesome at the club
Reverse Dom roles
Sex in public (again)
Have a foursome
Make a sex tape
Erotic Photo Shoot
Have phone sex/Skype Sex
Sex in a pool
Watch Porn together
Roleplay
Play Strip Poker (in Vegas)
Sex in an Elevator

“I think we can knock most of those out while we are here in Vegas. Or at least on our way.” He leans in close to me, whispering in my ear.

“Well, as soon as we are in the air, you have a whole half hour to accomplish the mile high club, because I am medicated, and will pass out.” I can't help but laugh, because it is the truth.

CHAPTER 15

A Vegas Surprise.
Three Days Later

"Where are we going, Levi?"

We step into an empty stretch limo, and it immediately pulls off, heading for the strip.

"It's a surprise." His fingers lace between mine, and thumb over the diamond that sits perfectly on the ring finger of my left hand. It is giant, impressive, and flashy. Everything I am not. Well, maybe impressive, but all of the others just don't fit me. When I returned from a lush spa day, I entered our penthouse suite only to find every surface covered with rose petals.

I never thought I would melt at the old cliché of rose petals, but between actually seeing it in real life, with my own two eyes, and smelling the rich floral smell, I loved every minute. Finally, I found Levi, after looking through almost every room in the place. He kneeled at the end of the bed in the master suite, a small blue Tiffany's box in his hand. My heart pounded so hard against my chest, I thought it was going to break through my skin and skip across the room.

"Seven, I never thought I would want to get married again. I never thought we would have anything more than sex. I can't even tell you how glad I am that you gave me a chance. This is quick, but clearly, we do things a little on the untraditional side. I know you are my forever. You and our baby. You own me; you have since that first night we were together. I love you, Seven James. Will you let me want you forever?"

Would I let him want me forever? How could I say no to that? Did I ever think I would get married? Hell no. But I didn't want to say anything but yes to Levi. So I did. I said yes. I promised myself I would start living, and that is exactly what I would do. Live. With this amazing man by my side for life, or until we kill each other in some kind of violent or bizarre sex act.

Now we sit in the back of the limo, and I wonder where the fuck this guy is dragging me off to. I cross my legs and the short black cocktail dress I have on rides up further. I hope wherever he takes me, I am dressed half way decent, although I could totally double as a street walker. Speaking of street walkers, I was so close to dragging Levi to the Bunny Ranch. I've always wanted to go. I mean, seriously, how can you beat legal prostitution? The women are fucking smoking too! He brushed it off with some excuse about me being pregnant and prostitutes not being the safest idea. Whatever, a girl can totally dream.

I turn as the car starts to slow, and we pull into a parking lot.

"You ready?" Levi asks as the car comes to a stop.

You have got to be fucking kidding me. "You are serious, aren't you?" I burst out laughing as I look out the window, seeing the sign that reads *The Little White Wedding Chapel*. He is serious as a heart attack too.

"You aren't leaving Vegas as Seven James." I laugh, because I know he is serious. I want to fight him on it; I really do. But I also want to leave Vegas as Seven Parker. Is that bad? Oh well. If it is, I do not give a single fuck.

"Well, Viva Las Vegas!" I take his hand and walk for the chapel. "I only agree to this if Elvis marries us."

If you enjoyed Hers,
check out this excerpt from
book two in the Hers series:

Sex is all I have ever known.

It started at an early age, and never stopped. Men, women, threesomes, foursomes, orgies. Fuck it, whatever goes.

Twenty-eight-years-old and nothing to show for my life but a fat bank account, and an impressive porn catalog. All featuring yours truly. Starburst Bloom.

I've met a crossroads, and I have a choice to make. I choose salvation. I choose life. I choose myself, for the first time ever.

I will find her. I will find the life I was forced to give up. I just pray that he stays out of my way.

PROLOGUE

Nearly eleven years ago

I look down at the crying newborn lying on my naked chest. It is warm, wet, covered in blood, and screaming, but I'm not bothered. This is *my* baby. This is the baby I have grown in my body for nine months. This is the baby I nurtured. I love it. I could never hate my own baby despite the circumstances in which it was created.

" Merry Christmas! It's a girl," the nurse exclaims, while they rub my daughter's tiny body down. Scrubbing all the fluids off of her. The cries coming from the baby turn into little whimpers and soon, she is rooting for my breast. Finding it with ease, she starts to suckle, and for the first time in my life, I feel love. I love this little girl more than life itself. I love my daughter. I love Willow.

As she nurses, I examine every feature on her plump little face. Her lips are full, cheeks are chubby and full, a small dimple graces the right side of her face, and as her eye lids flutter, I can see the smallest bit of blue leading me to believe she has her father's eyes.

Her father.

That fucking sack of shit.

All those years ago, I'd thought I loved Blue James, my best friend's older brother by thirteen some odd years. He was the bad boy everyone swooned over. I always thought it was a rite of passage to crush on your best friend's brother. When I was sixteen, he came on to me. We would mess around, but I always stopped it before it went too far. I was a virgin, and nobody knew I was completely in love with his little sister, and my best friend, Seven. She was my everything. My entire world. No matter what happened, she was there for me.

When Blue realized that there was more to our friendship than met the eye, he took what he wanted. He took my virginity. He didn't ask, or plead. He raped me. Took something I would have never given him. He led me to believe it was *my fault*. I had led him on, and a man so much older than me had *needs*. I couldn't mess around with him, without *finishing* him off. He was the first man I had been with, and the only man for a long time.

Now, the result of our on-again, off-again tryst lay in my arms, nursing at my breast. I want to cling to her, never let her go. But I know in two days, she will no longer be my baby. My parents, along with Blue's, found a couple, within the commune where we've lived for years, to adopt her. My Willow is going to live with strangers. It breaks my heart even to think about it, but I cannot raise her. Neither can her father. And while he might be an adult, I am merely a child.

She deserves a fair chance at life, not the careless, nomad existence I was raised with. Which is all I would ever be able to provide.

I run my finger along her cheek and continue to admire her features. She is the epitome of perfection, and I find it so hard to believe that I made her. She is a piece of me I will love forever. I keep telling myself I have agreed to give her up out of love. I just wish I would finally start to believe it.

The two days fly by in a blur of baby cuddles and visiting parents. Each time they visit the hospital, I hate them a little more. I hate that I can't pick up the phone and call my best friend, because the truth of the matter is, she has no idea I had a baby. I never told her I was pregnant. She would worry. She would leave behind her dream of college, and a career. I just couldn't do that to her. She means far too much.

He never came. Blue never shows at the hospital. He never meets his daughter, his own fucking flesh and blood. I thought I hated him over the years, but now what I am feeling for him must be exactly what hate is. How could you be so uninterested in your own child? But then again, he was just like his selfish parents, and mine. The apple really didn't fall very far from the tree.

My mother appears in the doorway, and a strange couple stands next to her; I know it is time. Time to let them take my baby. Time to let go of my dream of a happily ever after. The couple is older, early forties maybe. The woman has a warm and tender smile as she cautiously follows my mother. I cling to

Willow, holding her tight against my chest. My breasts ache from being engorged. My stomach feels deflated. My soul is on the verge of being gutted. Everyone in the room is smiling but me. Because I am the only one who is going to lose out.

"Star, this is Raine and Jeff Driscoll," my mother introduces us, but I don't look up from Willow's beautiful pouting face. The woman steps closer, and that is when I notice her striking green eyes; they are warm and loving. I can tell that look, because it is the look Seven has given me for the longest time. My defenses start to come down, because in my heart I know Willow will be taken care of, and loved. Unlike me.

I slowly place a kiss on her newborn forehead, and pass her to Raine. I don't want to watch them leave with her, but I have no choice. I swing my legs off the side of the hospital bed and creep across the room to the bathroom. I lock the door and turn on the shower. The tears come, and I hear the click of the hospital room door. I know my baby is gone, and I know I will never see her again.

I cry harder, and harder. I made a mistake. I want my baby back.

It is too late.

She is gone.

Dawn is a woman of many colors. Born and raised in the North-East, the youngest child of three, to two hard working, and extremely dedicated parents, she thrived on her love for creative writing; which started with the Narnia series. Her commitment to hard work lead her down a number of career paths over the years, stopping with her love for fiction.

Dawn is a mother, entrepreneur, and self proclaimed book whore; who enjoys whiskey, iPhones, and kink. She also loves to hear from her readers, so feel free to drop her a line anytime!

Where to find Dawn:

Facebook:
Facebook.com/authordawnrobertson

Twitter:
http:/twitter.com/eroticadawn

On the Web:
http://www.eroticadawn.com

Through email:
AuthorDawnRobertson@gmail.com

BOOKS BY DAWN

The Hers Series:
Hers
Finding Willow
Kink the Halls
This Girl Stripped
Seven's Diary

Other Books
Crashed
Take Me Out

Authored With J.M. Walker
Uncomplicated

Authored With Lily White
The Good Girl

Coming in 2014
Pursuit
Levi's Story
His
River

All books are also available on Barnes & Noble and iBooks!

Made in the USA
Charleston, SC
16 June 2014